Julia Green says:

'I wanted to go beyond thinking of teenage pregnancy as a problem. I was interested in exploring the complex feelings that surround any pregnancy, whether you are a teenager or not – the ambivalence you can experience even if you have made an active decision to have a baby. And I also wanted to explore motherhood itself – what it means to be a mother and the many different forms it can take in this most 'unmotherly' of societies in which we live.

There are thousands of young women who become pregnant in this country each year. Being a teenage mum is often a real struggle. But it isn't always a tragedy, because babies themselves are such a miracle: life-affirming, hopeful, with the potential to transform lives.

Julia Green lives in Bath with her partner and two children. She lectures part-time in English and creative writing, leads writing workshops for adults and young people, and works as a home-tutor for children who are not attending school. Blue Moon is her first novel for young adults.

Julia Green

Blue

MOON

PUFFIN BOOKS

PUFFIN BOOKS

Published by the Penguin Group
Penguin Books Ltd, 80 Strand, London WC2R 0RL, England
Penguin Putnam Inc., 375 Hudson Street, New York, New York 10014, USA
Penguin Books Australia Ltd, 250 Camberwell Road, Camberwell, Victoria 3124, Australia
Penguin Books Canada Ltd, 10 Alcorn Avenue, Toronto, Ontario, Canada M4V 3B2
Penguin Books India (P) Ltd, 11 Community Centre, Panchsheel Park, New Delhi – 110 017, India
Penguin Books (NZ) Ltd, Cnr Rosedale and Airborne Roads, Albany, Auckland, New Zealand
Penguin Books (South Africa) (Pty) Ltd, 24 Sturdee Avenue, Rosebank 2196, South Africa

Penguin Books Ltd, Registered Offices: 80 Strand, London WC2R 0RL, England

www.penguin.com

First published 2003
8

Copyright © Julia Green, 2003
An excerpt of the poem 'Libretti and Juvenilia' by
W. H. Auden, published by Faber and Faber Ltd, has been
reproduced by kind permission of the publisher.
The excerpts on pages 36, 76, 80, 108, 151, 165, 182 and
221 are taken from *Pregnancy and Childbirth* by Sheila Kitzinger,
published by Penguin Books in 1986. Reproduced here by
kind permission of the publisher.
All rights reserved

Set in 11.5/16 pt Adobe Sabon
Typeset by Rowland Phototypesetting Ltd, Bury St Edmunds, Suffolk

Made and printed in England by Clays Ltd, St Ives plc

British Library Cataloguing in Publication Data
A CIP catalogue record for this book is available from the British Library

ISBN 0–141–31535–0
ISBN-13: 978–0–14–131535–5

For Jesse and Jack

There was nothing to do in Whitecross; nothing there except a stone market cross and a straggle of houses, a petrol station and an off-licence, one grocery shop. The primary school had closed two years ago. Fields at the top of the lane near the church had been sold off for new houses, but none had been built. The fields stayed as they'd always been, only no one played there any more. The main road that went straight through the village was lined with tall lime trees that dripped sweet sticky stuff on to the pavement where Mia and her friends waited for the bus to the secondary school in Ashton. In the spring, they'd find the splatted pink mess of baby birds fallen out of nests in the lime trees. In the summer, the trees were smothered in pale yellow flowers and the sweet-scented air hummed with insects.

From Mia's house in Church Lane you could walk to the sea – not the sort of sea where people come for holidays, just a long strip of pebbles and, at low tide, a stretch of gravelly sand. The sea was too shallow to swim, and clotted with stinking seaweed. The tide left its trail of bottles and plastic, frayed rope and old shoes along the top of the pebble strip;

just occasionally it left a clutch of shells or the fragile skull of a seabird, scoured clean by the waves.

Above it all stretched the sky, a wide dome of pale blue or grey or milk white, filled with the thin cries of sea birds. In high summer, swifts darted and swooped with their sickle wings, and the air was filled with their high shrieks and screams until it was dark.

CHAPTER ONE

September 19th

'What's wrong with you this time?'

'I'm just tired, Dad. Need a day off school. OK?'

'No it is not *OK*, Mia. How can you be tired? It's only the second week back! How can you *do* this to me? I'm late already.'

'Well, just go then.'

'I can't *just go* and leave you like this –'

'I'm fifteen, Dad! You don't have to look after me.'

Mia turned away so he couldn't see her face. She felt sick again. She pushed past him on the landing into the bathroom and slammed the door. She could sense him still standing there, planning his next move. Her stomach clenched; the gagging feeling was coming again in her throat. She turned on the shower so he wouldn't hear her retching into the toilet. Even Dad wasn't *that* thick. He'd know. She wasn't ready for anyone to know yet. Not even Becky at school. Or Will. And especially not Dad.

Her guts ached; her mouth tasted sour. This was the third morning it had happened. Maybe she just had a bug or something. But her period was late. Each day she watched and waited, and it still hadn't started. More than two weeks late now.

Once she'd actually been sick it wasn't so bad. It left a hollow feeling, like hunger. She felt like that most of the time now, only she knew she mustn't eat much. She wasn't going to start getting fat.

Mia turned off the shower and rinsed her mouth at the basin. She cleared a space in the steamed-up mirror and peered at her grey mouth, white face, dark eyes. Her hair straggled, rats' tails. Becky was right; she should cut it all off.

Then the door banged downstairs. The whole house shook. The car engine revved up. Good. He'd given up.

Mia went slowly downstairs into the kitchen. She stood with her bare feet on the cold kitchen floor for a long time – minutes, hours – she didn't know. It didn't matter now – she had the whole day to herself. Through the window she noticed the garden, bright with early-morning sun. She felt a little surge of hope. Maybe things were going to be all right – her period would start today, and everything would be normal again. Outside on the lawn, a female black-bird stretched out its tail feathers like a fan. Mia smoothed her hands over her belly.

So quiet. So still. The house waiting. But there was an echo too, of the raised voices, angry hurting words dropped like cold pebbles. What if she'd told him right then? *I'm not going because I'm sick, and I'm sick and tired because I'm pregnant, Dad.* She imagined spitting the words out, bouncing them over the hard floor, translucent like marbles, each one with its coloured spiral trapped inside.

Mia took a small blue mug from the dresser and placed it on the table. As she filled the kettle the blackbird flew off in alarm. She opened the back door to let the cat in and then stepped right out on to the wet grass. The cold stung her bare feet, but she liked the feeling: sharp, more alive. She kept on walk-ing. Across the grass, through the gate, into the lane. The kitchen door was open behind her but she didn't stop, didn't look back. All the time she concentrated on her feet. Tiny, biting stones. Smooth tarmac, slightly warm. Mud, sticky, oozing up between her toes.

She was startled to hear a car slowing behind her. The woman from the big house up the lane gave Mia a strange look as she manoeuvred past. The whole village would have the news in ten minutes. *That girl.*

Walking along the lane with bare feet *at quarter past nine in the morning when she should be in school. But what do you expect with a family like that? A name like Mia!*

She pulled a blackberry off the hedgerow, but it was too sour to eat, the bobbles of fruit hard and tight. You shouldn't eat the berries from the lane anyway, Dad said. They were full of lead. *Poison.* When Mia and her sisters were small he took them across the fields to pick blackberries. She hated the way you had to stretch your hand through the fur of spiders' webs, and the way your fingers stained purple. You couldn't wash it off. It stained your nails like blood.

No blood. The blood still hasn't come.

Round the corner she saw something lying in the road. A dead seagull, one wing crushed open. The white feathers were smeared with the oily imprint of a car tyre. Just for a second, Mia felt she might cry. Her feet hurt.

The seagull is dead. No blood. Something wrong. My body. Waiting and waiting, and all the time maybe there's something growing inside me –

Mia stared at the dead bird. She couldn't leave it here in the middle of the road, to be run over again and again. Even if it was already dead. But she couldn't touch it with her bare hands. She pulled handfuls of grass and coarse broad leaves from the verge and used them to scoop under the bird's body, careful to keep her naked feet from treading too near. Close up it smelled. Of fish. Seaweed. Rotting meat. It was surprisingly large and heavy. Its glazed eye stared at her. She didn't feel sorry for it any longer. It was ugly and disgusting, a fat white body that stank. Only its wing, that fine skein of feathers; Mia did it for the terrible beauty of the crushed wing. She dragged the bird into the grass verge, and then gently folded the wing back over the body.

When she stood up she went dizzy for a second. She was cold, hollow with hunger. She still hadn't had breakfast. It must be nearly ten. She'd missed Maths. Becky would be wondering where she was, deciding who to be with at break. And Will? He'd be concentrating on *not* noticing her absence. Sitting about with Matt and Liam and the others. Talking films, in that pseudo-clever way they did together. Pretending not to notice the Year Eleven girls even though they were within spitting distance, sitting on the tables with their feet on the chairs in Room Ten.

She wiped her hands on the long wet grass in the verge. The seeds left dark oily marks along her palms, which wouldn't come off. She rubbed them on her legs. She could still smell the faint stink of fish, rotting flesh. It made her gag. Instinctively, she took the footpath away from the lane, down towards the beach. It wasn't a proper beach; just a long strip of stones at high tide with its line of washed-up junk, stretching as far as the village of Whitecross and beyond. At this end, it was usually deserted. She often came here by herself. And these last few weeks, with Will. The field next to the path, just above the beach, was where it had all started, those first few hot days at the beginning of the summer holidays.

She rinsed her hands in the sea and then sat down on the damp shingle. The stones hurt her feet, and a cold wind was blowing in over the water. She shivered, hugged her knees, but it was too cold to stay for long. In any case, there was nothing to do there. Nowhere to hide.

CHAPTER TWO

*T*he wet lawn was already beginning to dry. The kitchen door stood ajar, just as she'd left it. Mia rummaged through the bread bin and cut herself a slice of white bread for toast, spread it with marmite. The phone rang. It would be school, checking up on her. She should've phoned in sick as soon as Dad left. She ate her marmite toast slowly, letting the telephone ring. When it finally stopped silence washed back, like water filling the empty rooms. It's too quiet, Mia thought. She pulled out a chair and sat down at the table. There was a pile of unopened post propped up against the butter dish. Two letters for her older sister, Laura. She'd be coming home the day after tomorrow, before starting university. There was a postcard for the three of them from Kate, the middle sister, with a picture of lavender and sunflowers. Mia turned it over. '*Going further south,* *grape picking. Following the sun. See you!*' Kate's neat handwriting.

The phone rang again. Perhaps it hadn't been school after all, but something urgent. Dad? Will? She picked it up.

'Hello?'

Nothing.

'Hello?'

Silence, then a click. The empty line purred. Mia shrugged. Wrong number, probably. But her heart thudded. She snatched the phone up again and dialled one–four–seven–one. *'You were called today at ten fifty-three hours. The caller withheld their number.'*

A wasp banged against the kitchen window. Buzzed and bumped along the smeary glass searching for the way out. Stupid thing. Buzzing and angry, hitting uncomprehendingly against the transparent panes.

Mia dialled school.

'You should have phoned earlier.' The secretary's voice was sharp. 'Before nine thirty is the rule.'

Mia stuck her tongue out at the phone.

'And you'll need a note from your parents when you come back with reasons for your absence.'

Blah blah blah. Mia banged the phone back down.

There was shadow over the garden now. The day had lost its shine, its early morning promise. She

closed the back door and locked it and went upstairs
to run a bath.

She let it fill almost to the top, so that she could
lie almost completely under the water. Her sore feet
tingled. Gradually her body relaxed. She smoothed
her hands down her arms, her breasts. Her skin
looked translucent; there were faint blue veins she'd
never noticed before. Her hands hovered over her
stomach. It dipped, concave, between her hip bones.
Too thin, Dad said about her. '*You girls – obsessed
with it, aren't you? Bodies, diets.*' But she'd seen how
he looked at them, her friends, Laura and Kate's
friends when they stayed at the house; the way a sort
of gleam came in his eyes when he found them loung-
ing on the sofa in front of the telly. They flirted with
him, trying out their new powers, and he couldn't
help loving it, the attention from them. She knew.
She saw it all. Especially Ali. It made her pink with
shame.

Her mind floated as well as her body.

Will. His face. The way he looked at her. His soft
mouth on hers.

If he were here now. Her hands were his, moving
over her body, cherishing the detail. The pink coil of
a nipple, the way her belly button curved in, the tiny
white scar on her thigh where she had fallen out of
the apple tree when she was ten.

Lying in their field above the sea, watching the sun go down and the darkness creep over the field so that they were wrapped together in shadow. Will propped himself on one elbow beside her, his finger curling strands of her dark hair until it was bound so tight it pulled her scalp and she cried out, and then he bent over her, kissed her, so, so tenderly, and she thought she would die with happiness. That was where they had made love, the very first time.

Mia remembered it like a sequence in a film. She played it back, over and over. Sometimes she added bits or skipped the beginning. Maybe she was making it sound a bit more magical than it really was. Will, too much of the perfect, golden boy. She didn't care; it had felt like that, it really had.

August 4th

They'd started off with the others at the bus shelter, as usual, throwing stones at cans lined up in the main road. Mia sat on the kerb, her legs stretched out into the road. Heat shimmered off the tarmac even at nine in the evening. Occasional cars whizzed too fast along the main road, not slowing for the thirty-mile sign just before the village, and swerving out just in time to avoid the line of cans.

'Ciggie?' Liam offered his packet to Mia. She shook her head.

'Nah. You know I don't.'

Will didn't either. She was sitting next to him, his arm touching hers. They'd started going out together after half-term. She still couldn't quite believe it. Couldn't quite understand why he liked her.

Becky thought it was *because* she was so different. 'You know. You're a bit wild, and dangerous!' Becky laughed. 'And, of course, you look really good together – you so dark and him so fair.' Will's hair had bleached even more golden in the sunshine.

'Let's hitch a ride to Ashton,' Matt suggested. 'Get some cans and stuff.'

They'd been banned from the off-licence in Whitecross after Mia had tried to buy cider with her school lunch money. She'd said she was eighteen, even though it was obvious she wasn't. She barely looked fifteen. The woman behind the till had recognized her and telephoned Dad. More trouble.

'Do you want to go?' Will asked Mia.

She shook her head. 'No money. Think I'll just walk back home.'

'I'll go with you. We could go back along the beach?' Will suggested.

Becky and Ali smirked at Mia. She ignored them.

'All right.'

They crossed over the road together. Behind them, Liam and Matt laughed. Will's neck flushed. Neither spoke till they got out of sight of the others.

The moon was up already, even though it wasn't dark. The pebbles on the beach gleamed pearl-white. A man threw sticks for a black Labrador at the Whitecross end of the beach; each time, the dog splashed and then swam out, tail still wagging, found the stick, turned, just its head visible, like the sleek shape of a seal, then plodded back out with the stick, dropped it, shook. Water drops flew off its fur in a perfect circle of fine spray.

They walked further along the strip of beach. The tide was high. No one on the beach now. Will held her hand. Every so often he stopped, cupped her face in his hands, and kissed her. Mia felt a sort of fizzling inside. They didn't say much. It was usually like this. She couldn't think what to say. Will didn't seem to mind.

Will stopped to pick up a handful of stones. He selected a flat one, aimed and skimmed it over the water.

Mia counted. Five jumps. 'Show off!'

'You do it then!'

Mia chose her stone. It skipped the surface: five skips. 'There! You didn't think I'd do it, did you?

Confess!' She jumped on him, wrestled him down, laughing. He held her really tight and they walked like that all along the shingle, as far as the footpath sign.

'This is where my path starts,' Mia said. 'You coming?'

Will hunched down on the pebbles. 'Let's stay on the beach a bit longer.'

She sat beside him.

'Here. Shut your eyes and hold out your hand.'

He closed her fingers round a small pebble, warm from his hand. 'Now look. See how beautiful it is? Mottled blue, just like a blackbird's egg.'

It was beautiful, like he said, if you really looked. *A blackbird's egg.* She slipped it into her fleece pocket.

The sun had dropped right down below the hills across the bay. She huddled her knees under her dress, but they kept slipping out again.

Will stared at the sea. 'I love it here,' he said.

Mia had walked on this beach a million times. It was just stones, and the sea wasn't deep enough to swim unless you waded really far out. Along the top of the beach there was a dark line of stinking weed and all the junk left by the tide: plastic bottles, driftwood, bits of net and old shoes and tin cans. A mess. Nothing beautiful.

She tried to see it through his eyes. He hadn't lived

15

here as long as her. She'd never lived anywhere else, but he'd been all over the place. His family had moved two years ago from the city. He liked how wild it was here, how much sky. The fact that there was no one else but them. 'And all the different sea birds. Listen.'

Mia heard gulls; other birds she couldn't name. A flock of black and white birds flew together, piping a high, sad note over the water.

'Oyster catchers,' Will said.

Mia watched his face. She'd lived here all her life, but she'd never bothered with the names of things.

'Look! The moon's made a path on the sea.' She spoke without thinking. 'I used to want to walk on it when I was little. All the way up to the moon –' She stopped herself. Stupid. He'd think her stupid, saying that. Wished she'd said something clever, only she couldn't think what.

But he didn't tease her. He put his arm round her instead. 'You cold? You're shivering.'

She shuffled closer. 'My legs are freezing!' She rubbed them with her hands. Shouldn't have worn a dress. Only it had been so hot earlier, and she'd pinched one of Kate's to wear. Thin, and short and expensive. It made her look older. Will touched her leg lightly and then stroked it gently with the back of his hand.

16

'The wind's blowing in off the sea, that's why it's cold. We could go and sit in the field, if you like? It'll be more sheltered there.'

'OK. If you want.'

'It's too early to go home. Anyway, this is magic. Being here with you.' They kissed again. This time they took longer.

'See?' Will sat back from her. 'The moon's on your hair. You look all luminescent. Like those stones which give off their own light. You know?'

'No, I don't! You're weird, Will Moore!'

He shoved her so that she sprawled over, giggling, and then he pulled her up and she fought him back till they were both laughing. Together they clambered over the rocks at the back of the beach, up on to the grassy ridge that turned into the footpath.

There was a gap in the hedge that ran along one side of the path. They climbed through into the field. The hay had been cut some weeks ago; now the grass was short and dry. They sat down close together. Away from the sea, there was no wind at all. Grasshoppers still whirred and swallows dipped and dived for flies in the last of the evening light.

'See. It's warmer here.' Will took off his jacket and spread it on the grass. 'Let's lie back and watch for shooting stars.'

But soon they'd forgotten about the stars. And Mia wasn't cold any more.

She forgot everything. Where she was, what the time was, what she should have been doing. She hadn't meant it to happen. She hadn't planned it this way. She didn't think he had either.

They took off all their clothes. His warm body slid over hers, and all the time they kissed and stroked each other as if they were discovering something no one had ever found before. And then she felt something change in him and it was like something answered back from her, something wild and free. She felt as if she were flying. Free, like the swallows. Dipping and diving and swooping in the dying light. And that feeling changed again, and it was like a dark, greedy hunger for him that took her over completely. That was how they made love.

Afterwards they lay close.

'Are you all right?'

'Yes.' Her voice came out in a whisper. 'But – I didn't mean – what if –?'

'It'll be OK,' he said. 'Nothing's going to happen.'

She felt cold air rush over her as he moved away. The field was full of deep shadow. She struggled back into her dress. He turned away as he pulled his trousers back on.

'It was good, wasn't it?'

'Yes! Amazing.' Mia began to laugh.

'What's funny?'

'I don't know. Nothing. I just felt like laughing.'

Will sat next to her and pulled on his shoes. She bent over and kissed his head. His hair felt soft. Smelled musky and special. 'But you mustn't tell anyone what we did. No one. Not Liam or Matt or anyone. Promise?'

'Promise. You neither.'

'Right.'

Mia stretched her head back. The sky was dark and huge. 'I ought to get back home. My dad'll go mad if I'm late again.'

'I'll walk with you to your house, yes? And we can meet here again tomorrow? Or the next day?'

'OK.'

'Only if you want to.'

'I do! But we ought to be careful – you know – if we do that again.'

A shooting star whizzed across the velvet sky.

'See that?'

'Amazing, isn't it? How bright it is, and then gone. All burned up!'

'You get whole showers of them this time of year,' Will said. 'Meteorites, winging their way to earth.'

They watched the sky together, waiting for

another. Will smiled at her. 'Star-crossed. That's us.'

Mia puzzled over his words afterwards, lying in bed unable to sleep. Then she remembered. It was from the play – 'Star-cross'd lovers', from *Romeo and Juliet*.

Six weeks ago. She'd been full of joy and happiness at being close to Will. And they *had* done it again, but with condoms after that, so that this was so, so unfair. Just one time. The very first time ever. And then the waiting had begun, and the gnawing worry when her period still hadn't come. Then the sickness, and the hunger, and the exhaustion. Deep, wrenching misery filled her. Such a tiny amount of happiness, for such a short time. And now nothing could be all right ever again.

The phone rang again, then the answering machine clicked in with her dad's message. His voice drifted upstairs, calm and reassuring. But he wouldn't be like that with her. Not when he knew.

The bathwater was getting cold. Kate's voice drifted into her head. '*I don't like it when it's cold waves!*' Little girl voice. Kate, the middle one, having to share her little sister's bathwater. Kate was off travelling now, a whole year of it before university, and Laura had stayed on in Bristol most of the summer. After this next short visit, once Laura's term had started, there would just be her left. Her, and Dad. *And this – this thing inside her.*

Mia turned on the hot tap. She knocked the soap into the bath by mistake and it slipped like a fish in her hands as she tried to scoop it back up. She lay right back, head under the water so that her hair floated out like seaweed. Toast crumbs floated on the water. She'd stay like this all day if she wanted to. She didn't care.

Mia remembered the answerphone message after she'd got out of the bath. She went downstairs wrapped in her towel, hair still dripping. Might be Will. Probably not. Or Becky.

She pressed playback. No words came. Just the sound of someone crying. Soft, stifled sobs. Mia replayed the tape. It sounded like a child. Shivering, she switched the machine back on. The sound seemed to follow her upstairs. In the end, she lay on her bed with headphones on and drowned it out.

CHAPTER THREE

September 22nd

'*Y*ou think it's easy? Bringing up three girls doesn't come cheap, you know.'

'It's only twenty quid, Dad. No one else's parents make such a fuss about paying for things.'

'Not everyone else is struggling on their own with one salary and three growing daughters, that's why.'

'Well, that's not my fault, is it?'

As soon as she said it Mia wished she hadn't. Dad's face darkened. She saw the shadow wing across. Now he definitely wouldn't come up with the money.

'Tea, Dad?' Laura called from the kitchen. Impeccable timing. She must have been listening all the while. Mia watched her sister carry the mug and a plate of ginger biscuits over to their father's chair. Typical. The dutiful oldest daughter. But she didn't have to live here all the time, did she? She'd already escaped.

Dad started up again.

'It's a waste of money, Mia. If it were for books or a theatre trip or something for school it might be different. But an amusement park?' He spat the words out in disgust.

'Theme Park. It's a day out. Fun. Get it?' Mia glowered. 'But in our family it has to be education all the bloody time, doesn't it! Bloody education!' She slammed out of the room.

'Come back here, Mia! I won't have you swearing at me like that.'

She sat on the stairs, shaking. She could hear their voices – Dad's deeper tones and Laura, gentler. She strained to hear the words. 'It's her age, Dad. Don't be too hard on her.'

Mia seethed. Goody goody Laura. Talking about her as if she were a little kid when Laura was only five years older! Mia had forgotten how annoying she could be.

She swung the sitting-room door open again. Dad and Laura were sitting together on the sofa facing the open French windows. Mia stood in front of them, blocking out the light.

'It's not *my age*, thank you very much, Laura Zoe Kitson! It's just that I'm normal, unlike the rest of you. Normal, and wanting to have a good time like everyone else in the world except this – this *sad* family!' Her voice quivered slightly. 'And Becky and Ali and Will and everybody will be going – it's so unfair.'

Laura pushed past her into the garden. 'Horrid cat. It's caught something. Can't you hear?'

A thin shrieking sound filled the garden. Mia watched Laura chase after, then pounce on the cat, pin him down with one hand, tug at his tail. The cat squealed. She watched, horrified, as it dropped the crumpled body on to the lawn. For a second, the bird writhed, a broken thing.

Her stomach clenched. Throat gagged. *Oh no. Please. Not now. Not again.*

She ran upstairs, one hand cupped over her mouth. She flushed the toilet as she retched over it again and again. No one must hear. It left her shivering, exhausted. She rinsed out her mouth, splashed cold water over her blotched face. Tucked her hair behind her ears. The sour taste of bile coated her mouth. Finally she was ready to go back down.

Dad watched her from the hallway.

'You all right?'

Mia nodded.

He gave her his worn-down smile. 'You can have the money, the twenty pounds. You're right. You do need to have some fun. Look, we'll make a deal. You get yourself into school every day next week, no more days off because you're *tired*. I'll give you twenty quid.'

'Thanks, Dad.' Mia stepped slowly downstairs and planted a grudging kiss on the top of his head. 'See it as a bargain. I'm not going to be like Laura and Kate. I won't want to go to college or anything. Or do A Levels. You can save money on me!' One final barb.

She ran back upstairs and shut her bedroom door before he could answer back.

Mia lay on her bed. That smell. Dad's hair. It reminded her of Will. Will's hair smelled like that. Perhaps all men did. Comforting, but sort of *dangerous*. Weird to think Dad smelled like that as well as Will. She'd not noticed it before.

When Becky and Ali and Mia discussed the boys at school they sometimes asked her about her dad. They wondered why he didn't have a girlfriend.

'He's still quite good looking,' Ali said, one breaktime just before they broke up for the summer. 'Still got lots of dark hair, and the silvery bits are quite attractive.' She smiled her secret faraway smile. 'I rather like an older man. And your dad's interesting when he talks about books and stuff. And kind.'

'You should try living with him,' Mia said. 'You wouldn't say that then.'

Ali savoured the possibility. 'I wouldn't mind. If he

were just a bit younger. Pity he doesn't teach at our school.'

Becky and Mia snorted.

'Ali! Don't be so sick! It's Mia's dad you're talking about.'

'He's too tight with money for you,' Mia said. 'Mean, in fact.'

'Well, I suppose it's hard for him, without your mum there.'

'That's his fault too,' Mia said quietly. She took her feet off the chair and went to get a drink from the machine in the hall.

Mia lay on her bed, arms behind her head. The window was open; from the tree a bird called out its warning cry. The cat must have been let back out into the garden. *Apple Pie. Stupid name for a ginger cat. Mum's idea. 'He's sweet! Sweet as apple pie!'* she'd cooed over the small kitten when Mia and Kate brought him home in a cardboard box. The name had just stuck. That was over ten years ago.

Mia looked at Mum, smiling down from the photograph propped up on her chest of drawers. They were all in it. Mia, the littlest, sat on Mum's lap. She must've been about three. Kate and Laura stood behind, and then Dad at the back, one hand round each daughter, sort of holding them all together. It was taken in the garden. You could just make out the ash tree to one side. Smaller then.

'Stupid!' she said out loud. Mum still smiled.

Mia reached out and turned the photograph round. She didn't want to look at Mum's stupid face. Dad had found it for her, ages ago, and it had just stayed there, propped up against the jewellery box Kate had given her. They had other photos in albums downstairs, but in most of the pictures Mum was on the edge of things, looking as if she was thinking about something else. Mia supposed she was. Planning when and how to leave. Except when she finally did, it didn't seem planned at all . . .

An argument. Loud, angry voices. Six-year-old Mia stood in the sitting-room doorway listening to the voices slipping over each other down the dark stairwell. Fragments: '*How dare you! . . . everything of myself . . . nothing left . . . the children . . . you try it . . . really like . . .*' It was her mother's voice she could mainly hear, shouting, sobbing. The lower tones of her dad were less easy to make out. '*No . . . Can't.*' Once he yelled '*Alice.*' Mum's name. What was he doing? Should she go and see? Say something? Should she find Laura and Kate? They were still asleep upstairs.

In the background was the jaunty music of children's TV, which she'd switched on. She wasn't supposed to do that in the morning. She was supposed to read quietly or get her breakfast. Guiltily she switched it off and went back to the doorway. Listening. Her heart was thudding. Her feet were freezing. She rubbed one foot against her leg under her thin cotton nightie. Twisted her fingers through her hair.

The bedroom door upstairs opened; her mother spun out, downstairs, a flurry of clothing and hair and bags. Just for a second she hesitated, seeing little Mia standing there and then the front door was open, she was through, it banged shut. The car engine started. From the window she watched her mother drive away.

Afterwards, Mia used to wonder if she'd made it up, the bit about her mother pausing, hesitating. In any case, it hadn't been enough. Mia hadn't stopped her going.

Why hadn't she run after her? Banged on the window? Called her back? Maybe, if she had, everything would have been different. It was as if she had been frozen. Turned to ice.

CHAPTER FOUR

September 24th

'*M*ia. It's nearly nine thirty.'

Dad banged on her door again. 'Mia? Are you getting up?'

'Yeah. OK. In a minute.' She sat up and swung her legs round from under the bedclothes. For a second the room span; then it went back to normal. She got dressed and went downstairs to find Dad.

'OK. I'm ready.'

'What about breakfast?'

'Not hungry. I'll get something when we're there.'

Dad sighed heavily as he picked up his keys from the table. 'Let's go then.'

He'd only agreed to give them a lift because Becky's mum had phoned: '. . . Can you take them? I'd do it myself, but I'm working . . .' Mia, listening on the upstairs phone, had heard Dad explaining that he had to work most of the weekend too, even though he was at home: '. . . everyone always thinks teachers have short days, long holidays, but I always have to bring work home evenings and weekends. It's not easy, you know.'

Dad sounded pathetic, she thought. Whinging on about what hard work it was these days. Why didn't he do something else if it was so difficult? But he had agreed to drive Becky and her to Thornton Park. A major breakthrough. She hoped he wouldn't be too embarrassing in front of Becky.

He parked outside the entrance gates to let them out. 'OK, girls. Make sure you stick together the whole time. No talking to strangers.'

Mia grimaced.

'I'm not joking, Mia. There are all sorts of weirdos who hang out at these sort of places. You need to watch out.'

'What do you mean, weirdos?'

'Don't be obtuse, Mia. You know what I'm talking about.'

'Dirty old men in raincoats? For heaven's sake, Dad. You're the weirdo around here.' Mia raised her eyes in exasperation.

Dad turned towards Becky. 'Your mum will pick you and Mia up?'

Becky smiled sweetly. 'Yes, Mr Kitson. Don't worry.'

Mia cringed inside. Any minute now her dad would say something even more embarrassing. Sure enough.

'Less of the Mr Kitson, Rebecca. Why don't you call me David?'

Mia groaned out loud. 'Dad! Can't you just go?'

Becky clambered out of the back seat; Mia slammed the door and stalked towards the ticket office.

Dad leaned out of the window and gave a mock salute. 'It's been a pleasure, madam. So glad to have been of service. Any time.'

Becky grinned. 'Thanks a lot for the lift. Bye.'

Mia was determined not to turn round. Thank heavens Ali wasn't around to witness his performance. Or Will. She'd die of shame. Dad thought he was witty and amusing. He probably told jokes in class and thought the students saw him as one of them. Thank God he didn't work at their school.

Becky joined her in the queue. 'You shouldn't mind so much about your dad. He's sweet really.'

'He's just so – embarrassing. Your parents don't behave like him.'

Becky shrugged. 'Let's go and find the others. Forget about your dad.'

They went through the turnstile and walked on to the platform for the little train that took them into the park.

'How's things with you and Will?'

Mia shrugged. 'I don't know really. I've hardly seen him this last week.'

'Well, you're the one who's skiving, aren't you?'

'Ill, actually.'

'Oh yeah? Come off it, Mia.'

'Really.'

They'd reached the first rides. They stopped to watch three girls being buckled into harnesses for the SkyDive Experience. It cost extra, and they gave you a video of yourself afterwards. It looked fantastic, Mia thought. The nearest thing you could get to flying. You were winched up in your harness, way up in the sky, and then dropped so you free-fell through the air until the cable tightened, caught you, swung you up in huge, arching parabolas. The whole crowd held their breath as the girls waited, suspended high in the air. They held hands. Then they screamed, fell, seemed to hurtle towards the earth as if they'd smash into it and then, at the last moment, they were whisked back up and the smooth, high, swinging motion began. The screams changed note. Now the girls held their arms out and squealed with joy.

'We should do that. Only I don't have enough money,' Mia said.

Becky squeezed her arm. 'Never mind. We can do it another time. We'll get the money and come again. You, me and Ali.'

They found Will queuing with Liam and Matt and Ali for the WaterSlide. Mia's heart gave a little lurch. He didn't notice them at first; he was talking to Liam and they both laughed. Then Liam must've said something because Will turned round and smiled at her and Becky. Mia wished he'd hug her or something, but she knew he wouldn't, not here, not in front of his mates. Not cool. Well, she could be cool too, if that was what he wanted. They stood awkwardly in the queue.

Mia pulled a face at Becky. 'Shall we go on the slide together? Two in the same boat.'

Ali looked at Will. 'Good idea. Want to go with me?'

'OK.'

Liam nudged Matt and they both laughed.

Mia watched Will and Ali get in the rubber boat together in front of her and Becky. Will had to put his arms round Ali's waist in order to hold on. She felt tears pricking her eyelids.

'It doesn't mean anything,' Becky whispered. Then

it was their turn. Mia climbed in the round boat, Becky squeezed in behind, arms tight round her. They launched off.

The first part of the slide was a sheer drop. Mia's stomach lurched. She screamed; Becky squealed; then they were laughing, uncontrollably. They were skimming through the water, the boat spinning them round, and then it was over. Becky climbed out, still laughing.

'I'm completely soaked!'

Mia sat hunched in the boat.

'Mia?'

'I think I'm going to be sick.'

Mia staggered towards the toilet block, Becky tagging behind her. Out of the corner of her eye she saw Ali and Will climbing the steps for another ride on the WaterSlide.

They sat together at a bench opposite the House of Horror. Becky ate another doughnut.

'It wasn't that scary. Not enough to make you sick.'

'I wasn't frightened. Well, only a tiny bit at the start, you know, when it just drops away. I just threw up. That's all. No big deal.'

'Let's join the others then. Megaphobia next. Or that pirate ship?'

'Where's Will gone?'

'I'm not sure. They all went together, I think.'

'How *could* she?'

'Ali?'

Mia nodded.

'Typical really. She's like that. Don't take any notice. She's just jealous of you and Will. But he doesn't fancy her or anything. You can tell.'

They wandered over towards the biggest roller-coaster ride. A woman was standing her small children against the sign, measuring their height. 'See? I'm sorry. You're just not big enough, Mandy.'

The little girl began to cry.

Mia read the notice on the wooden post. *'Nobody smaller than this line may take this ride . . . No one with back problems . . . No one with heart problems . . . No pregnant women . . .'*

The words hit her like a fist.

No pregnant women.

Becky was saying something, but it was as if she were a long way off. Mia put out her hand to steady herself and caught Becky's arm.

'Mia? Are you all right? Are you sick again?'

Mia shook her head. She mustn't let Becky guess. No one must know.

'I don't think I'll go on this one. I'm starving. I'm going to get something to eat. I'll meet you later. I'll wait for you at the place where you can get your photo. OK?'

'All right. If you're sure. You should have had a doughnut with me earlier.' Becky ran off after the others.

Mia found herself a bench under a tree. Her heart was still thudding.

No pregnant women. That meant her. She mustn't ride on the rollercoaster. Presumably because it could harm a developing baby. Cause a miscarriage or something. The speed or the shock, or the rattling around and vibration in the cars. Made your blood pressure go too high or something. *You might lose the baby.*

She sat on the bench for ages, half watching the families milling around, trailing from one ride to another, queuing for chips or drinks or doughnuts, arguing, laughing, looking bored, while in her head the thought looped and circled like the rollercoaster itself. What if –? This was her answer, wasn't it? Why not? It was worth a try, surely?

She waited until she was sure Becky and Will and the others had gone far enough ahead in the queue for Megaphobia. She had to be on her own for this. What would happen? Would she feel anything? The rattling and shaking, the building pressure in her ears and belly and then – what? A sort of pop? A sense of things shifting, dislodging. That moment when it's all in the balance, teetering on the edge, and then the long slide down the other side.

Nothing would happen straight away. A day, perhaps, and then the bleeding would start, and everything would be all right. She could start all over again. She hoped it wouldn't hurt.

She walked past the sign and joined the queue. Above her, the rollercoaster looped and snaked its way through and above the trees. The screams of the passengers came in long waves, flooding out thought as she got closer to the front of the queue. Now it was her turn. Her face and knuckles were white, but there was no one watching. No one to witness her shaky descent at the other end, or to see the stooped figure retching into the toilet, over and over. By the time Becky and the others found her, she was sitting on a bench under the trees, composed again. Later, they all watched the firework display, and Will held her hand in the dark.

CHAPTER FIVE

September 28th

'*You may be feeling sick first thing in the morning . . . Your uterus is now the size of a satsuma. The baby has a head and trunk, and a rudimentary brain has formed. Tiny limb buds are beginning to appear. By the end of this week its circulation is beginning to function. The jaw and mouth are developing and ten dental buds are growing in each jaw.*'

Mia lay on the carpet in Dad's room, the book open on the floor. It was Mum's book. She'd left it behind in the bookcase, along with all the things she wouldn't be needing any more. Not in her new life, where being a mother didn't count. The book was called *Pregnancy and Childbirth* and Mia remembered looking at it before, as a little girl. She'd liked the pictures in it. The spine was creased and torn, as if her mother had read it over and over. A long time ago.

The baby. She hadn't thought of it as that, not really, not yet. She'd only thought about herself, and about telling Dad, and then, since the rollercoaster ride, she'd just been waiting, and hoping. But nothing had happened. It was still there, inside her, growing bit by bit.

Mia looked up. The cat was scratching at the door to be let out. She picked him up and nuzzled her face in his fur. He struggled to get out of her arms and scratched her in his scrabble to be free. Horrid cat. As a kitten he'd been the sweetest thing.

Four o'clock. Becky would be home by now. She dialled the number from the phone by Dad's bed.

'Becka? It's me!'

'You been skiving again?'

'Not really. I felt bad this morning – but I'm OK now. Do you want to come over?'

'I've got too much to do. We've got coursework essays for English and History. Honestly, Mia, you're going to have to catch up masses of stuff.'

'Don't you start. You sound like Dad.'

'Sorry. I missed you. No one to hang out with at break except Ali and she spends all her time chatting up Liam and co.'

'And Will?'

'Well, yes. If you really want to know.'

Mia felt tears welling up again.

'Are you still there? Mia?'

'Yes.'

'What's wrong with you then?'

'I dunno. I was really tired.'

'You're always saying that these days. Perhaps you've got glandular fever or something. Have you seen the doctor?'

'No.'

'Is your dad home yet?'

'No.'

'Do you want to come over? You could have supper with us. My mum won't mind.'

'OK.'

'Good. See you in a minute then.'

'What about your homework? You said you had to do it.'

'Stuff that. I'll do it later. Maybe.'

Mia chose a pair of black trousers from Kate's wardrobe. She combed her hair and then went through Kate's old make-up bag left lying on her dressing-table. Next to the mascara and lipstick was a small packet of condoms. Mia shoved it back in the bag. Sensible Kate. Kate never talked about boyfriends or sex, or anything like that. Imagine telling Kate she was pregnant! Or Laura. Or Dad. Or anyone.

*

Mia got her old bike out of the shed. Perhaps if she did lots of vigorous exercise? There was mildew on the saddle she had to wipe off with her sleeve and it left pale stains on her black T-shirt. It was uphill all the way to Becky's house. Just before she got to the white house on the bend she had to get off and push. The nosy old woman who lived there was in her garden, dead-heading roses and keeping an eye on the lane at the same time. She'd be pleased to have some more gossip about Mia to spread around the village. Mia kept her head down as she passed.

The door was open at Becky's. Mia left her bike propped against the garage and went in. Becky's mum was in the kitchen. She came to the doorway. 'Hi, Mia! OK?'

'Where's Becky?'

'Upstairs I think. You all right? Becks said you weren't in school.'

'I'm OK now.'

'Good. Lasagne for supper?'

Mia nodded.

'Expect you and your dad are missing Kate's cooking. Have you heard from her yet?'

'Just a postcard. From the south of France.'

Becky's mum sighed. 'Lucky her. While the rest of us –'

'I'll go on up then.' Mia escaped from the hallway. It was too hard, having Becky's mum all concerned and motherly about her. A bit of her longed to stay and linger in the warm kitchen, and be fussed over and taken care of. She felt her eyes brim. It wasn't fair. Why couldn't she have a mother like that? But there was no point thinking like that, was there? She thumped upstairs to find Becky.

Mia and Becky sat on the bed together, backs against the wall. Becky had done up her room like a shrine: candles everywhere, and mirrors on every wall, draped with silk scarves and bits of material Becky had picked up cheaply. Glittery stuff – pink and purple and gold – to make saris and stuff like that. Becky wanted to do Textile and Fashion next year, and then Costume Design.

'What've you been doing today then?' Becky asked.

'Nothing. Really boring. Tell me what I missed.'

'Well, the usual. Ali's been hanging around Liam and Will again.'

'What did Will do?'

Becky looked at Mia. 'He's too nice to everyone, Mia. He shouldn't encourage her. You know what she's like. You should tell her to keep her hands off him.'

'That's stupid. I don't own him or anything.'

Becky shrugged. 'No, but –'

'What?'

'Nothing. It's your business.'

'What? Say it. What you think.'

'Well, you're so laid back about it, it looks like you don't care. Get a grip, Mia. You just mooch about saying you're tired and kind of drifting.' She stopped abruptly, seeing tears rolling down Mia's face. 'Mia? I'm sorry.' Becky put her arm round Mia. 'Sorry, sorry.'

'It's not you, Becka.'

'Is it Will and you?'

'No – yes – sort of.'

'What then?'

'I think I'm pregnant.'

'Oh no! You can't be – you're not. You mean you and Will – you've been sleeping together? And you didn't tell me? Mia!'

She sounded impressed, as well as shocked.

'Becky, it's serious. My period's really late.'

'How late?'

'Three weeks – more.'

'*What?* Mia! But it doesn't necessarily mean anything. You can be late for lots of reasons – stress and stuff.' Becky was silent for a moment. 'Don't worry. I know what. We'll do you a test. Just to set

your mind at rest. You know, one of those kits.'
Becky began to smile. She looked quite excited. 'I'll
help you. We'll get one from the chemist's and –
I'll be there when you do it – and then we'll work out
what to do next.' She paused. 'Blimey, Mia. Why
didn't you tell me that you and Will were doing it?
What's it like? And *where*? Not at your house?'

Mia started to giggle. She couldn't help it. 'It just
sort of happened. In that field, near the beach, and
it was lovely, Becks. Really amazing. I know it was
stupid, you know, not using anything that first time.
I just had this feeling it would be all right.'

'You didn't? How could you be so stupid, Mia!'

'Don't be cross, Becky. It's too awful. No one
knows. You mustn't tell anyone. Please.'

'Well –'

'Please. I couldn't bear it.'

'But you need help, Mia. You know, proper help.
This could be really serious. Like doctors and stuff.'

'Not yet. Promise me you won't say.'

'Well. For now. OK. But you'll have to tell your
dad sometime, won't you? My mum would help.'

'No. No one. I shouldn't have told you, but I
couldn't not.' Mia started to cry. 'I'm so frightened.'

Becky hugged her tight. 'It'll be all right. You see.
You're probably not pregnant at all.'

But she wasn't convincing.

CHAPTER SIX

September 29th

'Mia?'

She stopped pretending to read and looked up.

'Can I have a word?'

Mia scraped her chair back noisily and put the book face down on the table, squashing the spine the way she knew would most irritate her English teacher. She slouched up to the desk by the window.

Miss Blackman lowered her voice. 'Mia, I fcel we should have a little talk. After school, today, in the English office. OK?'

'I'll miss my bus,' Mia mumbled through her hair. She wasn't going to look at her, with her sickly smile and her hair just so and that silly jacket and short skirt. When she sat on the desk to read to the class the boys said you could see right up it. She'd tried telling Dad about it, ages ago, and he'd got that funny look and said he always found Miss Blackman extremely pleasant and she was a very good teacher and that was what mattered, not what clothes she wore. But then he would, wouldn't he?

'Well, how about lunchtime then? Twelve thirty? It won't take long.'

Miss Blackman smoothed her hair behind one ear. New earrings, Mia noticed. Little gold stars with silver centres. On anyone else they'd look nice.

'OK. Can I sit down now?'

'Yes, Mia. But try and actually do some work. You're in a complete dream. And take that sulky look off your face please.'

Mia shrugged her shoulders. She'd like to hit her, her smug made-up face, and mess up her perfect hair, and shake her till the real person came out.

'What was that about?' Becky whispered.

'Stupid woman. I've got to see her at lunchtime.'

'What about?'

'Dunno. My *attitude* I expect.'

'I'll come with you.'

'Enough chat, Becky.' Miss Blackman was settling herself on the table ready to take them through the next chapter. She had her legs crossed. One pointed shoe dangled. The boys behind Mia were starting to fidget. Someone muttered an obscenity under his breath, but Mia heard. They shouldn't say stuff like that about women. She couldn't stand Miss Blackman, but even so!

At lunchtime, Becky and Mia waited at the doorway to the English office.

Miss Blackman hurried along the corridor, waving a pile of paper. 'Sorry, Mia. I can't see you now. It'll have to be after school instead. Three thirty.'

'She'll miss the bus!' Becky spoke up defiantly.

'It doesn't matter,' Mia said. 'I don't mind. I'll come then.'

Miss Blackman looked surprised. 'Thanks, Mia. Sorry. I've got a problem with some Year Sevens to sort out. Speak to you later.'

Becky and Mia wandered back up the corridor and through the swing doors. Their gang were lying out on the grass. They went to join them.

'What did she want then? A date with your dad?' Liam laughed.

Mia flushed angrily. 'Shut up. Mind your own business. Just 'cause you fancy her.'

'What, an old slag like that?'

'You're disgusting. I've had enough of you lot.' Mia stood up abruptly and stalked off towards the girls' toilets. She heard Will's voice, 'What's up with Mia?' and Becky's reply, 'I don't know. Ask her yourself. You're the one supposed to be going out with her.'

Becky came and joined her.

After French, last lesson of the afternoon, Mia and Becky walked slowly along the corridor to the English office. They waited outside the door for Miss Blackman to turn up.

'I'll meet you about four thirty then? Outside the chemist's?' Becky rested her hand on Mia's arm for a moment.

Mia nodded. 'Thanks, Beck. And don't say anything to anyone.'

'OK. Will was asking if you're all right. Don't you think you should say something to him?'

'No.'

'It's not fair, you having to worry on your own. It's his problem too.'

'Shut up. Not here.'

'OK. See you later.'

Miss Blackman's shoes clipped along the corridor. You could hear her a mile off. And smell the wafts of perfume. She smiled at Mia.

'Come in here, it's a bit more private. The cleaners will be starting on the classrooms any minute.' She unlocked the department office and turned a chair round for Mia to sit in. She stood, her back to the window.

'No need to look so anxious! But I am worried about you, Mia. We're Year Eleven now and this is a very important year for you. Last year you were hardly pulling out the stops, but this term so far you've done almost nothing. You're missing lessons. You have failed to complete any homework. You are already well behind with your coursework. It's all got to be done by Christmas, Mia. It's a substantial part of your final mark for English. I know you've heard this all before. But I want to get to the bottom of this. It's not as if you're stupid. You're just as bright as your sisters and they both got an A in English GCSE, didn't they? But they worked for it. It won't happen just by magic, you know.'

Mia watched Miss Blackman's perfect lip-sticked mouth. She stopped hearing the words. After a while they stopped echoing round the room. The room itself seemed to be going round so she had to clutch on to the sides of the plastic chair. She shut her eyes.

'*Waste of my time . . . no point trying . . . help . . . think . . .*'

Miss Blackman seemed to be getting more and more het up. Mia felt as if it was all happening far off, to someone else. Then she opened her eyes.

'Go on then, get your bus. I don't believe you've

heard a word of what I've been saying. I'll have to call your father, I'm afraid, and tell him how you've behaved here today. He'll be very disappointed in you, Mia.'

At last she felt something. Rage burned up through her guts. 'You keep your hands off my dad!' She hissed the words, and then she ran, out of the poky office and down the corridor and through the doors on to the driveway.

She was still furious when she got off the bus at the stop near the precinct. She slouched down the steps to the path that went along the river, kicking a bottle that someone had dropped on the path and smiling when it smashed against the stone wall. Fragments of green glass glinted among the nettles. She sat down on a bench near the river to wait until it was time to meet Becky.

A woman with a small child strapped in a buggy threw bread for the ducks. The child strained against the straps, squirming to be free, but the woman slapped his hand and he started to grizzle. The woman looked old and tired out. She shoved the bread bag away and got a packet of cigarettes out. Mia felt her anger flare up again. All that kid wanted was to run along the path and throw the bread himself.

She started thinking about Miss Blackman. Perhaps right now she was phoning Dad and he'd be going all gooey and smarmy and arranging to meet her so they could discuss Mia face to face. And then, in a minute, she and Becky would be buying one of those kits and soon she'd know for sure . . . only she knew already, didn't she? She didn't need some stupid kit to tell her. Waste of money. And then what?

The abbey clock chimed the half hour. She'd better run. She had to wait at the bottom of the steps for a crowd of men in suits. A youngish man in naff pin-stripes winked at her. 'Cheer up, love. It might never happen.' Stupid prat. It made her want to throw up.

A thin ray of sunshine came through the clouds, and for a moment she forgot to be angry, and noticed the river instead, how it looked almost beautiful. There was the usual muck floating about still, but a swan bobbed just under the bridge, its wing feathers fluffed up in an arc above its body. And something else caught her eye. There was something on the parapet of the bridge. Mia's heart thudded under her ribs. It was someone – a child, she could see now – balanced on the edge, just above the river. Mia looked around. No one else seemed to have noticed. The crowd of suits had passed on down the path, their backs to the bridge now; the woman with the buggy had gone too. The small figure crouched there, as if it would jump at any moment. Should she yell out? She might startle the child and it would lose its balance . . .

Mia ran up the steps, two at a time, and then round on to the road that went over the bridge. For a minute, the bridge itself was out of sight. As she came on to it she saw immediately that the child was no longer there. Heart still thudding, she peered over the edge. The river flowed smoothly round the stone bridge supports. The swan bobbed, preening its wing feathers. An old tree branch swung round in the eddies of water near the bank. No sign of a child. And there had been no splash. She would have heard that, surely? Even when she was running up the steps. The child must have climbed back down, and run along the road in the other direction, back towards the shops. But so fast? It seemed unlikely.

She was out of breath by the time she got to Becky.

'Sorry! This weird thing just happened.'

Becky listened to Mia telling her about the child.

'Perhaps you just imagined it. Or it was the light or something. How would a little kid get up on the edge of the bridge anyway? A teenager, maybe. People sometimes jump off the parapet into the river in the summer, when it's hot. But it's really danger-ous. You can hit your head on the stone bits. And if you get swept into the weir you've had it. There's nothing you can do, anyway. Forget it. Let's go and get your kit.'

'Not yet. We could have a drink in the market first? And have a look round the shops. Please, Becks?'

Mia dragged her feet. She wished she hadn't arranged this with Becky. It didn't seem like a good idea any more. Suppose someone saw her? And once she'd done the test . . .

It was busy in the chemist's. They stopped at the make-up section and sprayed on the expensive perfume testers until the assistant asked them what they wanted to buy. Then they moved through toothpastes and shampoos, past eye-care and feminine hygiene to the pregnancy tests.

Mia wanted to walk straight past and out of the far exit, but Becky dragged her back.

'Look, you've got to do it. Come on. No one's watching.'

Mia looked round anxiously. It was true – no one was paying them any attention. The nearest woman was filling her basket up with boxes of tampons. Mia shifted nearer to first aid and alternative medicines.

'Blimey! Loads to choose from!' Becky was enjoying herself.

Just looking at the pink and blue packets made

Mia feel sick. In the end they chose the cheapest one, which could be done any time of the day.

'Perhaps we shouldn't bother. It's a waste of money.'

'You can't not do it now, Mia. Unless you want to do a free one. At the doctors. I got you a leaflet.' Becky unfolded the coloured leaflet from her pocket.

'Where did you get that?'

'School medical room. You know, where the school nurse goes. They've got loads, about smoking and drugs and Aids and stuff.'

'Suppose someone saw?'

Becky giggled. 'They'll think I'm pregnant then, won't they? But no one did. It was after school. Here, you have it.'

'I don't want it.'

'Don't be daft. Shove it inside your bag. In your planner or something. No one's going to go through your bag, are they? Not even your dad's that nosy.'

'He might.'

'Well, you'll need to tell him sooner or later, won't you?'

'Not necessarily.'

'Come on. Let's buy this one and go and do it.'

'Where?'

'Your house?'

'OK.'

They chose the check-out with the doziest-looking cashier. Mia gave Becky the ten pounds she'd taken from Dad's stash behind the clock that morning before school. It had been easy to take it; she wondered why she'd never done it before. All those times they'd argued about money – she could have just helped herself. He was so busy with work he'd probably never notice. Tonight he had to do an Open Evening for new pupils at his school; he wouldn't be back till after nine. She walked out of the shop and waited for Becky outside. They stuffed the plastic carrier into Mia's school bag and went to get the bus back to Whitecross.

Becky phoned her mum on her mobile.

'I'm at Mia's, Mum, to keep her company. Her dad's got a meeting. I'll be home about nine thirty. Yeah. We'll do homework together, here. Yeah. Pasta or something. It's fine.'

Mia listened. Lucky Becky. It really wasn't fair.

'We'll cook first. Then we'll do it, yes?'

'I'm not hungry.'

'You have to eat, Mia. Don't be so daft. I'm starving, anyway.'

They cleared the pile of letters from the kitchen table. Dad hadn't got round to opening them.

Mia knew instantly the handwriting on one. She hid it behind the clock to look at later.

Becky filled a pan with water for pasta.

'Right. The ceremonial opening.'

They spread the instructions out on the bathroom chair. Mia's hands shook.

'You have to wee in this one and then we add this little tube of stuff and wait. Just three minutes.' Becky took off her watch and placed it on the chair. 'It's like Miss Matthews' science demo.'

'Go out then. I'm not doing it with you here.'

'Call me when you've finished.'

Together they watched the seconds tick round.

'No peeping till the three minutes, OK?'

But Mia already knew.

'Maybe it's wrong? A false positive?'

Mia shook her head. 'Good try, Beck. But it's true. I'm pregnant. Official.'

'What are we going to do?'

'I don't know.'

'But you can't have a baby, Mia. You're fifteen.'

'We'd better get rid of all this before Dad gets home. Help me tidy up.'

'We can't put it in the bin. What if your dad sees?'

'Wrap it in something. Put it in the dustbin outside. He's not going to go through that, is he?'

'You're so . . . cool about it, Mia. Are you all right?'

'Course I'm not. I'm pregnant, aren't I? There's a baby growing inside me.'

'It's not a baby yet. You mustn't think like that, Mia.'

'Why not? It's true, isn't it?'

'It's just a bunch of cells or a blob of jelly or something.'

'I don't want to talk about it any more, OK. Not tonight. I'm really tired, I need to go to bed.'

'What are you going to do though, Mia? We've got to talk about it.'

'Not now. I just want to be by myself. Just go, Becky. Please.'

'Oh, but I don't think –'

'Please. I'll be OK. Don't worry. I need to sleep.'

'Can't I just stay till your dad's back?'

'No. Just go. I'm sorry, you've been really nice, Becks. I'll see you tomorrow.'

'Are you sure you're OK?'

'Yes.'

'I'll be off then.'

'Thanks.'

'Bye, Mia.'

*

Mia went into the bedroom. She lay on the bed in the dark room. She was cold. It felt like a stone was inside her belly – hard and cold and ready to drag her down under the water. She thought briefly of the child on the bridge, the sun on her hair, the swan floating on the water below. She thought about Will – how distant he seemed now they were back in school. She never saw him alone. He was always with Liam or Matt. Or Ali was hanging around. He hadn't phoned her, but then she hadn't phoned him either. She supposed she'd been waiting for him to make the next move. And he hadn't. What did that mean? Were they still going out?

She switched on the bedside lamp, went over to her bag and found the leaflet from Becky. The words made her eyes water; she couldn't take them in. She'd read it tomorrow maybe. She was too tired now. And tomorrow she'd phone Will. And she'd work out what she was going to do. She curled up on the bed, knees hunched up, spine curved round.

CHAPTER SEVEN

*S*he must have gone to sleep because next thing she knew Dad had come back from his meeting and was standing in her bedroom doorway.

'Well?'

'Dad? What time is it?'

'Are you going to tell me yourself?'

The cat had sneaked into the bedroom and now jumped on to her bed, purring loudly. He paddled his paws on her stomach, claws out. Dad waited, fingers drumming on the doorpost. His face was very red. This is it, Mia thought. He knows.

'What are you talking about? What time is it? I didn't hear you come home.'

'It's nine thirty-five p.m. I've just got back after an exhausting evening to find a message on the answerphone from your English teacher telling me you're skipping lessons and failing coursework and extremely ill-mannered when she tries to talk to you about any problems. Well, madam? What have you to say? As if I haven't got enough on my plate. I get in from work at this time of night and find this – this –'

'This mess? Me? Is that what you mean?' Mia sat up, shoving the cat on to the floor.

'Just tell me what's going on, Mia.' For an awful moment she thought he was going to cry.

But he switched on the light and that started him off again. 'What *are* you doing? Sleeping fully clothed, still in school uniform. You've left the kitchen filthy, nothing washed up. I found the doors all unlocked. I suppose you had that boy round here again?'

The anger began to burn in her guts again. How dare he!

'What's the point? You never listen. I don't have to talk to you.' Mia pushed past him out of the room. He tried to grab her arm, but she shoved him hard, knocking him back against the door. He swore under his breath, shocked at the sudden pain in his shoulder. Mia was running now, down the stairs, across the hall and, without thinking, she was opening the front door, slamming it behind her, running across the grass, through the gate and into the lane. She heard him calling out behind her, calling her name, but it was too late now. She ran on into the darkness, down the hill, not knowing where she was going except away, away from him and the house and school and everything. She sobbed as she ran, so it hurt her chest and she had to slow down. But she kept on going, as if by instinct, towards the sea, and the footpath, and her field. Will's and hers.

It was cold without a coat. And so dark. No moon or stars tonight. It began to drizzle. A wind blew in from the sea. She turned off the lane just in time: car headlights, the sound of tyres on damp tarmac. Dad, coming after her? She skirted the mud and felt her way down the familiar track to the gap in the hedge. Something rustled in the hedgerow and then the dark shape of a large bird flapped slowly from the big trees away over the field. Her heart thudded.

Now she was safe in the field. He'd never find her here. If only she'd brought a coat or a rug or something. The drizzle had turned to a steady, penetrating rain. She crouched in the shelter of the gorse bushes, where patches of bare earth felt almost dry, until her heart had stopped its wild beating.

In the distance she heard a car grinding up the hill. Dad going back? He'd be going upstairs, into her room, expecting to find her safely returned. Mia groaned out loud. Becky's leaflet, half stuffed under her pillow! He was probably looking at it right this minute.

She couldn't go back, not now. But she couldn't stay here. She couldn't bear to turn up at Becky's house and have to tell her mother everything. It would be the first place Dad went to look for her. She wasn't going to make it easy for him. Will's? His parents wouldn't mind. She might be able to avoid them altogether. What would Will think, her turning up now? Where else could she go though? She'd have to risk it.

There were lights on in every window. No curtains drawn. Will's older brother was silhouetted in one of the upstairs rooms and two people moved about in the kitchen, crossing back and forth in front of the window. She waited in the darkness, shivering with cold, then crept round to the side of the house and threw a handful of gravel against Will's bedroom window. After the second shower of gravel, his face peered out, puzzled. He opened the window a little and saw her standing in the shadows.

'Mia? Wait there. I'll come down.'

She watched the front door open, a strip of light spread out on to the gravel path, the dark shape slip through the gap.

'Mia? What are you doing here this time of night?'

She started to shake.

'You'd better come in. You're soaked!'

'What about your parents?'

'They won't mind. They're in the kitchen anyway. They don't have to know. I'll smuggle you upstairs if you like.'

Will shut the bedroom door quietly and they sat down on the bed. He looked at her critically.

'You look terrible. Your hair's all wet. And you're all muddy. What've you been doing?'

'I ran away.'

'You're joking! Aren't you?'

'I dunno. I mean, I ran out of the house and I'm not going back. I've had enough.'

'What about your dad? He'll be really worried.'

'I don't care. I hate him.'

'What's he done now?'

She bit her lip so she wouldn't cry. It had been a mistake to come here. How could she possibly tell Will? He looked so – so young and innocent sitting on his bed, him all clean and golden-looking next to her with her dark ragged hair and thin white face and muddy clothes. It had been a shock to see his room. His history essay was spread out on the wooden table under the window; he must have been working on it. His saxophone case lay open on the floor.

'He doesn't hit you or anything, does he?'

Mia shook her head. 'It's not that. He's not violent or anything.'

'What then?'

Mia shook her head. She was close to tears. She longed to tell him and have him put his arms round her and say it would be all right and he'd help her. But she knew it was hopeless. She couldn't even begin to say.

'I can't explain. He just came home late and started up again, going on and on at me. All that stuff about school –'

– *and, oh, Will – I'm pregnant and it's the end of everything – I don't know what to do –* But the words stuck in her throat.

He looked at her, uncomprehending. She knew it was impossible for him to understand. There he'd been, playing music in his room after a cosy family supper, calmly working on his essay, his parents laughing downstairs, and then she arrived, like a stray dog or something, out of the blue – cold, wet, in tears – impossible.

'Do you want to stay here tonight?'

'I dunno. Can I?'

'Well, I guess so, but what about your dad? He'll be going mad. He might phone the police or something. You have to tell him you're OK.'

Mia felt suddenly furious at the unfairness of it all. She turned on Will. 'You phone him then if you're so concerned about him. On your mobile.'

'No way, Mia! Have you gone crazy or what?'

'I don't want to speak to him, Will. Can't you get that?'

'You have to, if you don't want him sniffing around after you, with police and social workers and the lot. He'll look for you at Becky's, and then here, won't he? So just tell him you're safe.'

'All right. Stop going on. You're starting to sound like him. Give it here.'

She dialled the number, held her breath, let out a sigh as the answerphone cut in.

'Dad, I'm staying at a friend's for the night, so don't worry about me and don't come looking for me either. I'll see you tomorrow after school, OK?' She quickly cut the line dead before he could pick up the phone.

It was a relief to have done it. Now she felt hysterical giggles rising. Will looked so – so serious, and scared. She felt a hundred, million years older than him. Braver, harder.

'What's so funny?'

'You. Like a little boy. Like you're going to be in trouble!'

'Well, I've not had as much practice as you!' He

gave her a shove and they fell together on to the bed, stifling laughter.

'Sshh. Someone will hear! Look, I'll go down and tell them I'm going to have an early night. Then Mum won't come in.'

'Can't you lock the door?'

'If I can find the key.'

Mia listened to the noises in the house while Will was downstairs. His brother was playing music in his room; she could feel the thump thump of the beat. Someone crossed over the landing and went to run a bath. Will's footsteps came back up the stairs, two at a time. She looked into the mirror on his wall and tried to smooth her wild hair with his comb. He came back in, flourishing a key.

'I nicked it from Ben's room. Same lock as this door.'

They lay back on the single bed together. Mia's shoes left muddy stains on the cream cover.

'We'll have to turn the light off so it looks like I'm asleep,' he whispered. 'We should have done this before. Smuggled you in. It's easy, isn't it? And much warmer than our field.'

'I like our field.'

'Yeah, well, I did too, but that was summer.'

Any minute now. In the darkness. She was going to tell him. She rehearsed the words in her head.

Will, I'm pregnant, neutral tone. *Oh God, Will, something awful's happened*, tragic tone. *Will, guess what*, sort of bright, I-can-cope tone. None of them sounded right.

'Shall we get under the covers? Get undressed.' Will's whisper sounded loud in the darkness.

'Yes.'

Mia sat on the edge of the bed and pulled off her muddy shoes, wriggled out of her skirt and tights, pulled the black school sweatshirt over her head. Naked, she crept to the window and pulled the curtains slightly apart.

'Mia? What're you doing?' Will hissed. 'Are you mad? Suppose someone sees you?'

'It's too dark. I don't like it so dark. It's just a tiny chink, no one will see.' Mia crept back under the covers with Will. Her skin felt cool next to his. They put their arms round each other.

He doesn't know. Inside me. His baby as well as mine. Ours.

The strip of grey light through the curtains revealed the soft shadows of his bedroom. His things. Books and CDs and old junk – rocks and fossils, model aeroplanes he'd made when he was ten or eleven, a music stand. She could just make out the title of a piece of music propped open: 'Blue Moon'.

They listened as one by one the different family

members went to bed. When finally the house was completely silent, everyone asleep, Mia crept into the bathroom to use the loo and wash her tear-streaked face. She longed for a hot bath, warm clean towels, someone to tuck her into bed. Now she lay next to Will. The first time they had spent a whole night together. It was strange, being warm and close like this, but still not saying. Not telling him what was happening inside her body right now.

'Do you want to do it? Make love?' Will's whisper sounded loud in her ear. He stroked her back and for a moment she felt comforted. 'It's OK, you know, I've got a condom in the drawer.'

Too late for worrying about that, she could say. *Should have thought of that right at the beginning.*

'Not here,' Mia said. 'It doesn't feel right. Not with your parents just down the landing.'

Will sighed. He went on stroking her back though, and it wasn't long before she turned round and kissed him, and his hands moved round to her breasts and then down over her belly and between her thighs, and then it was easy, and delicious and exciting and somehow comforting to Mia – quiet, gentle lovemaking so that no one would hear.

After it was over Mia lay next to Will, staring into the dark, arms wrapped around her own body.

She couldn't tell him because she knew already

what he would say. Because she couldn't bear to see the look of horror and panic spread across his face. The way he'd withdraw, retreat, reject. This hadn't been part of the deal. And what could he do? Maybe his parents could cough up the money, if she needed money. Though she couldn't imagine how he'd tell them. And soon it would be all over Whitecross. *That girl. In trouble. Again. But what did you expect? . . . The mother left them you know.*

Lying in the cramped bed in the darkness, Mia knew she was alone really. Will couldn't begin to understand her. She didn't even want to try to make him. Tears dribbled down her hot cheeks and soaked the pillow.

CHAPTER EIGHT

September 30th

'There's a message for you, Mia. Your father will collect you from school at three thirty and would like you to wait at reception. OK?'

Becky and Mia glanced at each other. Mia rolled her eyes. She'd told Becky everything at break. She'd had to explain her muddy shoes, and why she hadn't brought her bag with all her books and stuff. She had been sick before school again this morning. She and Will had got up really early, left his house before anyone else was up. They had breakfast in the transport cafe on the main road. Will paid. She'd thrown up the whole lot in the school toilets.

After English, last lesson of the afternoon, Mia dragged herself towards reception and the main entrance doors. No chance to do a runner – Dad was already standing by the noticeboard, pretending to read the newspaper clippings. He must've got off early, to be here at three thirty. He looked terrible, Mia thought. His hair was all sticking up and dishevelled where he'd run his hands through it. Her heart started to thud. What was he going to say about last night? Just at that moment Miss Blackman appeared. She dangled a key on a piece of string.

'I've got us the counsellor's office,' she said, smiling towards Dad.

Mia scowled. 'What's going on?'

'Thought it would be useful to have a third party. For our chat, Mia. Since you won't speak to me on my own. And Miss Blackman kindly agreed to assist us.'

Miss Blackman smiled again. Stupid woman, Mia thought. Pushing her way in like this. It was nothing to do with her. They must have planned the whole thing. And lied about it. Dad must have phoned her last night. It was outrageous.

Miss Blackman gently closed the office door and indicated to them to sit down. Mia perched on the edge of the low chair, her head hanging down.

Miss Blackman started first. Her voice was soft, condescending. 'We're *very* concerned about you, Mia. We've noticed you're not . . . well, happy at the moment. Not your usual self. I know things came to a bit of a head last night. Your father was very worried. Did you think what *he* might be going through? Running off, out all night – and you're just fifteen!'

She leaned forwards towards Mia, who shrank back. 'We understand it's hard for you without your mother at home, and both your sisters have left now, I believe? But it's affecting your school work and that threatens your whole future,' Miss Blackman hesitated, 'and we wondered, Mia, well, your father did, whether there was something more serious we should know about?' Embarrassed, Miss Blackman looked towards Dad.

He took over. 'Last night after you ran out I found this – and I wondered, Mia?'

With horror, Mia saw that Dad had tears in his eyes. He fumbled in his pocket and then held out the crumpled leaflet towards her, his hand shaking. 'Is – is this it? The trouble? Because if it is, you need help, Mia, and you need to talk to us.'

Teenage Pregnancy – the Facts. Becky's leaflet. *This was it, the moment she'd been dreading for days and days. Dad knew.*

Mia hunched over, refusing to look at either of them, stomach churning, about to be sick.

'Shall we assume then, since you won't deny it, that it is?' Miss Blackman, too, had gone pale.

'Please. Say something.' Dad leaned forward in his chair and put his hand on Mia's knee.

The touch made her anger flare again. It was almost a relief to feel it, the familiar rage burning inside her at the unfairness, the injustice of it all. All she could think of now was escape. 'Don't touch me! I don't have to listen to this crap!' She knocked the chair flying as she stormed out of the room. Her head pounded. She let the school doors bang back violently as she ran up the drive towards the bus stop. A small group of girls were standing around there, watching her. She felt her face flush. She bit hard on her lip so she wouldn't cry. The sick feeling rose in her throat. She heard the school entrance doors swing back and Dad's footsteps running up the drive behind; now she was trapped between him and the bus-stop crowd. He grabbed her arm.

'Get in the car.'

She didn't resist. She went with him to where it was parked in the road, leaned against the door while he unlocked it, and crumpled into the front seat. He sat still for a moment, staring ahead, then he started the engine. He turned towards her.

'Tell me it's not true, Mia. That you're not – pregnant.'

He spat the word out. Like he was disgusted by her. Would like to spit her out too.

She couldn't stop the tears now. Not even when she bit down so hard she made her lip split and blood

oozed in a thick bubble. She licked it with her tongue.
She stared straight ahead. Two boys on skateboards
glided gracefully past on the road.

'I am.'

He leaned forward, collapsed his head on to his
arms on the steering wheel. When he sat up again
his face was grey. Mia's hands shook in her lap. She
was cold all over. This was worse than anything
she'd imagined. She thought he'd shout and storm at
her. Not this icy silence. The car engine revved and
throbbed. Still he sat there, unmoving. His eyes were
blank when finally he looked at her again.

'Who was it? That boy you've been seeing? From
school? Will?' He could hardly bring himself to speak
the name out loud. 'Well? Speak up, Mia. I can't hear
you. I'll kill him – the irresponsible bloody mindless
idiot. What does he have to say about this? Eh?'

'He doesn't know,' Mia mumbled through hot
tears. 'I haven't told him.' The tears started to run
down her face.

'You stupid, stupid girl.'

He jerked the car into gear.

They drove past clumps of schoolchildren walking home, laughing, mucking about, kicking stones
along the gutter. Two Year Ten girls waved at Mia
and then turned to each other and laughed at some
private joke. For everyone else it was just a normal

afternoon; they'd walk home and turn the telly on and get something to eat, and everything would be as it always was. She was utterly alone in the world. She wished she'd told Will. That he was here now.

With a jolt she realized that instead of turning towards Whitecross as usual, Dad had taken the main road, into Ashton.

'Where are we going, Dad?' Her voice came out thin, frightened.

'Ashton General Hospital.' His eyes were fixed on the road. 'Been here before, seen it all before. Every year at my school there's some stupid girl in trouble in Year Ten. Or Eleven. Didn't expect it to be my own daughter. Thought you had more sense. Intelligence.'

He wasn't like Dad any longer. He was a grey man, made of steel. Ice in his heart.

'So I'll take you to the hospital and they can sort you out.'

What did he mean? She was too scared to ask.

She'd be sick any minute. There was the sign for the hospital, and then the mini roundabout, and the road that went into the hospital. Instead of going the usual way, towards Accident and Emergency and the main ward entrance, he was turning left, to the car park signposted Maternity and Antenatal.

The minute the car stopped Mia opened the door

and was sick into the gutter. Dad waited till she finished, then without saying anything, he gripped her sleeve and steered her across the tarmac towards the hospital entrance.

Now Dad sat next to her in the crowded waiting room of the Early Pregnancy Diagnosis Unit. The woman at reception had told Dad where to take her. She hadn't listened to what he'd said, too busy trying to stop herself being sick again. Two other young girls sat huddled with their mothers. One had spiky blue hair and a lip swollen with rings and studs; the other had shiny dark hair, perfect make-up, lovely clothes. The mother with her, in an immaculate linen suit, leafed through a *Vogue* magazine so fast that Mia knew she wasn't really reading it. There were young women with husbands, and several with a troupe of noisy children in tow. The men looked embarrassed. Mia wondered what it would be like to sit here next to Will. How young he'd look, how impossible. Even so, she wished he was. Holding her hand. Telling her it would be all right.

Dad sat two seats away from her; he'd brought his briefcase in from the car and was reading a pile of papers from school. His face was still red with anger.

The nurse took away the form Mia had filled in with her name and address and date of birth. She had to put down the date of her last period. That was easy; the date was etched on her memory now. Next she had to have a scan, and that would tell them how pregnant she actually was. Depending on that, they would arrange for her to have a medical or a surgical termination. That's what they called it. They'd already given her a leaflet explaining what happened. That was after the first meeting, in a little room with plain walls and just three chairs. A woman in a white coat explained everything. So much talking.

'You have three options,' the woman said. 'You can have the baby – at fifteen! Imagine! You can carry the baby to term, then have it adopted; you can have a termination.'

The nurse, or doctor, whoever she was, explained how bad it would be for Mia to have a child when she was so young. 'You are still a child yourself,' the woman continued. 'Already anaemic. And much too thin. Are you perhaps mildly anorexic? Anyway, you couldn't possibly manage.' The voice went on and on. 'You have your whole future to think of. Your whole life ahead. What sort of life could you possibly give a child?'

Eventually Mia stopped hearing anything. Something small and precious inside her felt like it was curling up and dying.

*

When it was Mia's turn for the scan, she went into the consulting room alone. It was dark. It felt horrible, the way they made her take off her things and lie on the couch with her knees up. An *internal* scan, they said. *The latest technology*. She tried to strain round to look, but the screen was turned round so she couldn't see. She wasn't supposed to see, the woman said. Afterwards, she had to get dressed again and sit at the desk to see the nurse.

The nurse turned a cardboard dial of dates and numbers. 'You're about nine and a bit weeks, going by the measurements and your dates.'

The nurse continued to talk. *Measurements*. Mia was remembering the page in the book at home. She'd looked at it yesterday: '. . . *just under an inch (2.5 cm) long . . .*'

'Do you understand? Too late for the medical method, where you have to take pills; that has to be before eight weeks. So it has to be surgery. It's very straightforward. The actual operation doesn't take long, but you have to have a general anaesthetic. You can go home the same day. I know it's all very distressing, but don't worry. You've read the leaflet, haven't you? Have you any questions? Anything at all.'

She was trying to be kind.

'I'm not sure,' Mia mumbled through the curtain of hair.

'What, dear?'

'I still haven't decided. Not yet.'

'Oh. I thought we'd been through all that already.'

'But I'm not sure. What to do.'

The nurse gave a tiny sigh. 'Shall I get the counsellor back?'

Mia shook her head. 'I want to think about it, at home.'

'You haven't got long, you know. The earlier the better. If I booked you in today I could probably get you a bed in two weeks, given your age. They try to accommodate girls like you. But if you leave it, I can't guarantee a booking – you'd have to go private instead of NHS – and it's getting late, you know. The earlier the better. You understand that, don't you? Shall I get your father in?'

'No.'

'Take the leaflets. Talk to someone at school. Your teacher maybe. You can ring this number to speak to the counsellor.'

'OK. Can I go now?'

The nurse sighed again. 'Yes. But don't forget. There's not much time.'

This was awful. Worse than she could ever have imagined. Why wasn't Will here with her? It wasn't right that she was all alone.

Dad, stony-faced, watched her as she came back into the waiting room.

'Well? Is it settled?'

'No. I haven't decided.'

She saw anger flush his face. Hers flared too, to match it.

'I'm phoning your mother the minute we get back. Perhaps she can talk some sense into you.'

'She can piss off. She doesn't care about me anyway. And don't tell anyone else. How dare you tell that woman!'

'You watch your language. Don't you dare speak to me like that! I don't know what's happened to you, Mia. Your attitude. This whole thing is just – unbelievable. I can't believe it. That I'm here with my own daughter – who is fifteen, for heaven's sake. How could you do this, Mia?' He took a deep breath, trying to keep control. 'What have I done to deserve this? How could you be so bloody stupid?'

'*Ssh*. Keep your voice down.'

'Don't you shush me, young lady. You wait till we get home!'

Dad gathered up his things and started walking out of the unit. All the other people waiting seemed to have gone quiet, watching them.

Mia tried to keep up. 'Don't tell anyone, Dad.

Please. Not Kate or Laura, or anyone, I can't stand it. Please?'

He stopped for a second and looked at her pleading face. 'I am trying, Mia, to understand. It's the pits, isn't it? For you, I mean. I admit I am very shocked – and I am very, very angry. *That boy –*' his voice trailed off. 'But – you're my little girl. The baby of the family. I'm *trying* to think about you – what's best for you.'

Mia winced. That word. *Baby.*

They turned the corner of the corridor. They had to cross through the Antenatal Clinic now, to reach the exit. Two very pregnant women stood at the desk. A toddler pushed his buggy into the back of his mother's legs. 'Ouch! You little beast!' She smacked his leg and he started to cry. Mia pulled a face at him and he stopped bawling for a minute in surprise, then started tugging at his mum's skirt.

Mia pushed through the doors into the car park. It was raining. She trailed after Dad, oblivious to the huge puddles spreading over the uneven tarmac. She sat in the car with soaked feet, silent. When Dad leaned over to turn on the radio she flinched, as if she thought he had been about to hit her.

CHAPTER NINE

October 4th

'You may notice changes in your skin because of the pregnancy hormones in your system . . . The baby's limbs are developing very rapidly, and fingers and toes are beginning to be defined on the hands and feet.'

Mia fished the envelope from behind the clock and held it over the kettle to steam it open. She'd done it so many times before she knew exactly how long to hold it before it went soggy and the writing ran.

This time, there was a different address at the top. Bristol.

Dear David,
Sorry it's been a while. Lots happening here, as you'll see from the new address. We moved in at the

weekend and already it feels like home. We've started decorating already and the sitting room looks lovely – cream walls, pale carpet and sofa covers, deep blue curtains – books and flowers everywhere, like I always wanted. There's even a garden! Not big enough for an ash tree, like we had at Whitecross, but I think I might put in a Morello cherry, for the blossom. It's a bit late for planting stuff, but I'm going to put in loads of bulbs for the spring – snow-drops and narcissi – whites and creams. It will be lovely. We'll be having a bit of a party next weekend and you could come if you wanted? Bryan's fine about it. Bring the girls, of course – if they want to come.

Hope all's well. I had a postcard from Kate, some-where in France. She says they're going further south, with the grape harvest, then on to Italy. No doubt she's already told you. You must be thrilled with her A Level results. As I am, of course. I think a gap year is a very good idea.

One of the good things about the move is that I'll be able to see Laura much more often. I'm not intend-ing to cramp her style. She won't want me around her when she's busy being a student! I won't have much time anyway, with me being full-time at the Centre at last. However, the odd cup of tea together – it'll be more like a normal mother–daughter thing. We've lots to catch up on. Maybe now they are leaving home it will be easier for them to see me.

It'll be strange for you and Mia, just the two of you left at home. I hope she's not too lonely. Tell her we've got a spare room now so she'll be able to come and stay some time if she wants to, although she probably won't, knowing her! I suppose it's probably hardest of all for her, because she was so little when I left. She's always so angry about everything. Even when I try to talk to her on the phone –

The awkward silences, the heavy sighs, Mia's moods. How's school? *Boring.* How are you? *All right.* Would you like to meet up? *No.* Tell me what you've been doing. *Nothing.*

That was what Mum meant. Why she'd stopped phoning. If only she'd picked up the phone that day when it had rung and rung. Perhaps that had been Mum, sensing that Mia was in trouble, needed her. You heard about that, sometimes, didn't you? A sort of telepathy between mothers and children.

Bryan is planning a special holiday for us –

Mia screwed the letter up in sudden disgust.

It was staring her in the face, Mia realized. The evidence. Why didn't she just face it? What kind of mother was she, living far away in Bristol, with a new man and a new house and a new life? It was obvious really. Mum didn't want anything to do with her past life in Whitecross, or with Mia, did she? She was starting all over again, with her lovely garden and her white cushion covers. Mia was nothing but a problem. And now a *pregnant* Mia?

The trouble with having time off school was that she was on her own too much. Dad didn't have a clue. He'd cooked up this stupid plan with Miss Blackman, which was supposed to mean Mia got lots of rest and there were no pressures on her. She wouldn't have to explain anything at school: they would say she had a virus. Afterwards she could come back and get on with her work and her life and no one need know anything.

Afterwards.

She wouldn't think about that. Not now.

Mia dressed slowly. There were hours to fill. She stuffed a pile of dirty washing into the machine and turned it on. It hurt to bend: her jeans cut into her stomach. She found another pair in Kate's room and put those on instead. She must be eating too much. All that pasta and toast. Better get some more healthy stuff. Fruit. Bowls of grapefruit and oranges and seedless red grapes and plums. That's what she needed. Just the thought made her mouth water. She picked up the money Dad had left on the table for the shopping and went out.

She was almost as far as the village when the Shoppers Special bus rattled past her. A crowd of people were waiting at the bus stop: market day. The last two people were getting on as she reached the stop; without thinking, Mia got on too. She might as well hang out at Ashton. More to do than at Whitecross, anyway. She kept her head down so no one would speak to her. The heating had been turned on; it blasted her legs from under the seat. The bus lurched and jolted along the narrow lanes and the voices of the passengers welded in her head so she felt sick.

'All right, love?' The driver tried to catch her eye as she got off. 'Have one on me!'

What did *that* mean? Fat slob! She hated the way men did that, made stupid comments, looked you up and down like they wanted something. Mia slipped through the crowded bus station towards the precinct.

There were the usual market day crowds – blokes selling off cheap stuff, seducing the female shoppers with their banter, two thin lads playing the guitar badly and singing out of tune, two young women setting up their pitch. Mia watched them spread out an Indian bedspread and boxes of beads and cotton thread. The dark-haired one put out two hand-written signs advertising *Hair Braids* and *Temporary Tattoos (not henna)*. She smiled at Mia. 'Want one, love?' Mia shook her head. She lingered for a while, looking at a beautiful embroidered bag with sequins and beads and tiny mirrors stitched in. Becky would love it. From time to time the woman smiled at her. Eventually she wandered on. There was nothing to do if you didn't have any money. It was the same everywhere.

She watched three small boys with crew cuts and trainers sliding on the smooth precinct floor outside the supermarket. Their mothers were arguing about something. They didn't look much older than her really. They turned away from each other and shouted at their children to follow. The children shouted back. One had chocolate all round his mouth. Mia walked on towards the steps at the far end.

As she approached the end of the covered precinct, Mia suddenly noticed a little girl. She hadn't been there seconds before, Mia was sure, although the way she was standing, one leg resting on the wall, leaning up against it, made her look as if she'd been standing for hours, waiting for someone. Her fair hair was all dishevelled, spread out round her head. She was wearing a thin cotton dress, no socks, trodden-down sandals. She looked vaguely familiar.

Mia gave her a faint smile. The girl stared back. Then she turned and started to walk out of the precinct towards the river. Mia walked after her, slowly. The girl looked over her shoulder at one point. Mia stopped, waited, then followed on. She didn't know why. It was something to do, wasn't it? The child was too young to be by herself, Mia thought. She couldn't be more than about seven or eight. And she looked cold in that thin dress. Old-fashioned. No coat or even a jumper.

The child walked over the bridge. Mia followed behind. Halfway across, the child stopped. She leaned against the parapet, stretched her arms up to pull herself higher so she could see over the edge. Mia's heart began to thud. So that was where she'd seen her before.

This time, the girl lowered herself down again and walked on over the bridge to the steps that wound down to the river bank.

She was waiting at the bottom. Mia hesitated.

'You're following me.' The child's voice was thin and reedy.

Mia shook her head. 'Not really. Just walking.'

The girl waited, as if Mia should say more.

'I saw you before, didn't I? On the edge of the bridge.'

The girl looked pleased.

'I thought you might fall.'

The girl shook her head. 'I never fall.'

They walked along the river bank to the bench. Mia sat down. The little girl crouched by the railings, watching the water. It swirled and raced today after the rain in the night. Mia shivered again.

'Aren't you cold?' she asked the little girl.

'Yes.'

'Why don't you wear a coat then?'

'I don't have one.'

'Why not?'

She didn't answer.

Mia tried again. 'What's your name then?'

'Lainey.'

A long silence. Mia finally offered: 'I'm Mia.'

A branch bobbed and swirled along on the current. Then an empty crate and a plastic sack. The branch snagged itself on the overhanging plants and caught there. It made a sort of dam, trapping bits of rubbish as they floated downstream.

'What're you doing then, Lainey?'

'Nothing.'

'Shouldn't you be in school?'

'Shouldn't you?'

Mia laughed. 'I've got time off, for real. I'm not skiving.'

'Why?'

'I'm having a baby.'

She listened to her own words hanging in the cool air. They'd come out by themselves. A little slice of truth. She felt lighter for letting them out.

'I've got a baby,' Lainey said.

Mia looked at her in surprise. 'What do you mean?'

'I've got a baby. At home.'

'Oh. Your mum, you mean. A baby sister.'

'It's a boy.'

'Brother then.'

'Not a brother.'

'What then?'

'Adam. He cries all night long. Cries and cries and cries.' Lainey straightened up. 'I'm going now. See you tomorrow.'

Mia watched her skipping along the path until she disappeared from sight. It felt lonely without her, suddenly.

I'm having a baby. She'd said the words out loud.

But she wasn't, was she? She was too young. It would mess up her entire life. She couldn't possibly look after a child. They didn't stay sweet little babies very long, did they? Crying babies grew into difficult

*toddlers and demanding school kids and they cost
you money and you never had any fun ever again.*

Last night, Dad had made her sit with him at the
kitchen table. She wouldn't look at him. She hated
him, the way he went on and on. How stupid she was.
How irresponsible. How thoughtless. *Remember that
book she'd read at school? Those kids had to carry
about a bag of flour the weight of a baby and look
after it as if it were real. It was supposed to make you
realize what it meant, being responsible for this baby.
All day. All night.*

*Well, this was it. The real thing. And she might
as well get on with it. Making her mind up, that is.
Yes, of course she had a choice. Well, sort of. It
would be better if she made a proper choice, not drifting along like she usually did. But what were the
options really? Honestly, Mia. This is not the time to
start making silly statements about your choices.
How could you possibly bring up a child? You can't
even look after yourself. Who is going to pay for it?
That sixteen-year-old boy? With a paper round or
something?*

What could she do? Even with her hands over her
ears she couldn't shut out his voice. On and on. And
when he said he was going to go straight round to
Will's house and tell his parents, she couldn't take
any more. So she'd finally said yes. And he went

straight away and phoned the woman at the hospital. They'd given him the date for the termination.

Afterwards she could go back to being the old her. Mia. Whoever that was.

She waited on the bench by the river to see if Lainey would come back, but she didn't. She'd better get the shopping and then the bus back to Whitecross before everyone came out of school.

CHAPTER TEN

October 11th

Lainey was waiting for her the next time she got the bus into Ashton. As the bus turned into the bus station Mia glimpsed her hovering by the flower shop, and then when she walked down the precinct Lainey was at the same spot as before. She had on a red jumper today, hand-knitted, like something from a charity shop, and old-fashioned leggings. Mia waved.

'You're late. Seven days late.'

'Sorry. I didn't say I'd be here. I can't come in every day. Where do you live then?'

Lainey shrugged. 'My house.'

'Don't you ever go to school?'

Lainey pulled a face. 'Stop asking me questions.'

'OK. Sorry. Are you hungry? I just thought – well – it's cold. We could go to a cafe.'

'If you want.'

'I'll pay. I've got money from my dad today.'

They perched on stools in the covered market cafe. Mia ordered hot chocolates and a bacon sandwich for Lainey. The little girl looked tiny, legs dangling from the high stool. She shouldn't be out on the streets like this. It wasn't safe. Close up, her face looked older than Mia remembered.

'How old are you, Lainey?' Then she remembered about the questions. 'Sorry.'

'My turn.'

'OK.'

'When are you having your baby?'

'Oh.' Mia's voice came out small and scared. 'I'm . . . not.'

'Why not?'

Mia buried her face behind a curtain of hair. 'I can't,' she mumbled.

'Why not?'

Mia was silent.

'But you said. You said you were having a baby? How can you not have it then?' Lainey was persistent. 'Where will it go? Will you give it away?'

'You go to hospital. They take it away.'

Lainey looked confused. 'And then where does it go?'

'Shut up, can't you?'

Lainey waited just a few minutes. She swung her

legs against the wooden stool and hummed. Then she started up again. 'Won't it be sad, the baby?'

'It's not a baby yet. It's just a sort of blob. It doesn't feel anything.'

'How do you know?'

'Shut up!' Mia snapped.

She sipped the hot chocolate. It was sweet and comforting.

They sat in silence together for a while. Lainey huddled over the counter top, her fair hair tangled over her arms. Eventually she looked up at Mia.

'My baby's sick,' she said. 'I'll bring him next time to show you.'

'You can't do that, Lainey. Not on your own.'

'Why not?'

'You're not old enough. It's not your baby anyway.'

Lainey wouldn't speak after that. She didn't drink her hot chocolate or eat her bacon sandwich. In the end, Mia had both. She was starving. She watched Lainey slide off the stool and go and stand at the jewellery stall where a woman was choosing earrings. She called out to her.

'Lainey? I need the loo. Wait here. I won't be long.'

But Lainey had disappeared by the time she got back. Mia wandered around the town for a while, looking for her. She went over the bridge and along the river path, then back to the precinct and the high street, but there was no sign of Lainey. It began to rain, cold, slanting arrows of wet that pierced her thin jacket and turned her hair into rat's tails. She still had the shopping to get.

Until this September it had always been Kate's job. She liked cooking; Mia didn't. This morning, before he left for work, Dad had opened the fridge and the kitchen cupboards and issued instructions to Mia, sitting at the kitchen table with the list. 'Pasta, baked beans, eggs, bacon, wholemeal bread, digestive biscuits, cheese, potatoes –' and Mia had added her own things: oranges, grapefruit, plums, grapes, chocolate. In the end they decided the list was too long and Dad said he'd go to the supermarket after work with the car, but he still gave Mia twenty pounds, just for a bit of fruit and vegetables and bread. He'd gone soft about money the last few days. And softer with her too. Treating her like she was made of glass or something. At supper he'd tried to tell her about when Mum was pregnant with Mia. 'Sick as a parrot. Not just in the mornings either. Exhausted. Couldn't manage the girls. Or cooking, shopping. Nothing.'

'Shut up, Dad.'

He'd looked hurt. Stupid man. Didn't he understand *anything*?

He ate the rest of his dinner without talking, except to ask her to pass things. Pepper. Tomato ketchup.

Mia didn't want to hear him talk like that about Mum. He made her feel worse. Like Mum hadn't wanted her even then, before she was born. Or maybe it was Dad? Or both? Maybe she'd just been an accident? And it was the last straw, and six years later Mum had finally had enough.

Mia stopped on the wet pavement for a moment. Instinctively, her hands clutched protectively over her own belly. *I'm sorry.* Not out loud, but inside her head she spoke her first words to the little blob growing inside. *Sorry, little bean.* That was how she imagined it. A small bean nestled in a silk-lined pod. Like the broad beans Dad used to grow when she was little. Fat green pods sprouting off a straight stem. The flowers like black and white moths. You slit the pod to find the row of bright green beans snug in the white furred lining. Plucked them out.

CHAPTER ELEVEN

Mia walked aimlessly along the high street. It was still pouring with rain. She stopped for a moment to shelter under the blue awning at Brenda's Hair Salon. Through the big glass windows she watched two women cutting hair. A girl with spiky bright orange hair swept up the curling strands from under the chairs. Mia watched her. Next she brought a cup of coffee to the woman sitting nearest the door. Mia noticed the squashy-looking sofa, and a pile of magazines on a low table, like someone's sitting room. It looked comfortable and inviting. Why shouldn't she go in and have her hair cut? Becky had been going on at her about it for weeks. It would be warm and dry, somewhere to be for the next hour. Mia pushed open the door.

Self-consciously she removed her wet jacket and tucked her dripping hair back behind her ears.

The orange-haired girl looked up. 'Can I help you?'

'I'd like my hair cut. Please.'

The girl flipped open the large appointment diary on the table. 'When d'you want to come in?'

'Can someone do it now? Straightaway?'

'Sam? Can you do this girl next?'

Mia found herself being led upstairs to have her hair washed. She closed her eyes. The water was warm. The girl's hands scooped her hair into the basin, smoothed and lathered it. She chattered all the time. Mia didn't bother to answer or even to listen. She let her head rest, kept her eyes shut, let herself drift in the babble of sound. She felt safe and cosy. Someone else was washing her hair, taking care of her. She didn't have to do anything. She didn't have to think.

Back downstairs, Sam and Mia looked together in the mirror at Mia's hair.

Sam combed the lank strands over her shoulders. The comb bit and tugged at the knots and made Mia's eyes water. Sam laughed. 'You haven't done this for a while, have you?'

Mia frowned.

'Well, what shall we do?'

Mia stared at her pale face, dark shadowed eyes. She looked terrible.

'I want it all cut off. Really short.'

'You sure?' Sam held the hair back tight behind Mia's head, trying it out. 'It would suit you. Show your face more. You've got lovely eyes.'

Sam worked quickly, quietly. She didn't ask many questions and Mia was grateful. She watched in the mirror as the scissors snipped round her head, and swathes of dark, wet hair cascaded to the floor. The orange-haired girl brought her a cup of weak coffee and she drank it even though she didn't really like the taste. Perhaps it would be like this in hospital. She could lie in a clean bed and nurses would bring her drinks and stroke her head and whisper that everything would be all right. She could give herself up to it. There would be an anaesthetic and she could drift into sleep and not have to think any more.

'There. What do you think?' Sam held the small mirror behind Mia's head.

Mia peered at the strange sight of her own neck, the edge of her shoulder bone, the neat spikes of hair. No one would recognize her.

She smiled at herself in the mirror.

There was no money left for the shopping. She walked slowly back towards the bus stop, glancing at herself in the shop windows she went past. If she'd had more money she'd have bought something new to wear too. It was a long wait for the next bus. She might as well go back down to the river. The rain had stopped. Lainey might be there by now. She could show off her new hair.

But the river path was deserted. Lainey must have gone home. The rain, probably, had forced her back. To wherever it was. Probably one of the estate houses at the edge of the town. Mia imagined a shabby semi-detached house with pebble-dashed walls and a scruffy front garden. And the sick and crying baby. Lainey's wrung-out mother, pale and desperate with rings round her eyes from no sleep and too many fags. That's what she imagined. But maybe not. Maybe Lainey's mum was at work and that's why she didn't know Lainey was running wild round the town, never in school. Lainey didn't ever talk about her mum. Or her dad. But then neither did Mia, did she?

She sat down on the wet bench. Her neck was freezing. Two overweight men in tight suits walked by along the path. They stared at her. One said something she couldn't hear, and they both laughed. No hair to hide behind. She glowered back. It was starting to rain again. The church clock struck. There were another fifty minutes to kill before the afternoon bus was due. Becky and Will and everyone were cosy in school, getting on with their lives. It wasn't fair.

Nothing was fair. She was all alone. Tears mingled with the rain on her face. There was just her, and little bean. And soon there wouldn't even be little bean.

CHAPTER TWELVE

*W*ill was standing at the bus stop. Her heart pounded when she first caught sight of him, leaning against the shelter, his white school shirt unbuttoned at the neck and his tie half mast. And she felt a weird mixture of things – pleasure, fear, something else she couldn't name. She saw the shock of recognition on his face as she stood up to get off. And then he grinned.

She stepped off the bus on to the pavement in front of him.

'What're you doing here, Will?'

He shrugged. 'Got a lift back with Mum. She dropped me off. What's all this about you being ill then?'

Mia flushed.

'You don't look ill. You look fantastic. Your hair –'

Mia's hand reached up self-consciously to smooth down the spikes.

'So how come you're off school officially? As opposed to your usual skive?'

She started to walk away from the bus stop. 'Not here. We can't talk here.'

'Why not?' He caught her sleeve.

She ignored his question. 'How come you knew I'd been to Ashton?'

Will shrugged. 'Dunno. Just a guess. What've you been doing?'

'Hanging out. Getting my hair cut. Talking to this girl.'

'Who?'

'She's just a little kid. But I keep seeing her – hanging around town, or by the river – there's something wrong – something odd about her.' All the way home from Ashton Mia had been thinking about Lainey. It wasn't right, a child her age on her own like that all day; anything might happen to her. And that time she'd seen her on the bridge. It was dangerous. She could've fallen in really easily and only Mia would have seen.

Will wasn't interested in her talking about Lainey. 'Do you want to stay here or shall we go back together?' He put his hand on her arm and the touch made her shiver.

'Mia? Are you OK?'

It was hopeless, carrying on like this, Mia thought. She had to tell him. Becky thought her ridiculous, that she hadn't already. She'd gone on about it over the phone to Mia. '. . . Why shouldn't he take some responsibility? It's his fault too. He ought to have to think about it too. It's not fair . . .' Mia had found it too difficult to explain. That there wasn't any point. He couldn't help her.

'What's wrong, Mia?' He was persistent. Perhaps he knew already. Perhaps Becky had finally said something. And it was all round Year Eleven. *Guess what? You know Mia's away . . . well . . .*

'Can't you guess?' Mia spat out the words.

'Becky said something about a virus, and Ali – why are you looking at me like that?'

'I can't believe you're so – so – thick about some things.' Mia started walking, fast, down the main road.

'Wait!' Will ran after her. She kept walking, but he caught up with her and together they watched in silence for a break in the traffic so they could cross. A white van screeched to a halt as Mia dashed out into the road. Will grabbed her arm and ran with her. The van driver wound down his window and swore at them.

'Mia! Do you want to get us killed or what!'

Mia half ran, Will tagging after her. Couldn't he see how upset she was? Why didn't he just leave her alone? Go back to Ali or whoever he fancied now she wasn't around at school? Without thinking, they both turned off the main road down the lane that went to the sea.

The beach was deserted; not even dog walkers had ventured out along the wet pebbles that afternoon. The tide was still high, just going down. The line of flotsam and jetsam stank with its new deposits.

'I'm pregnant, Will. Did you really not guess?' Mia turned her damp face towards his. She saw at once that he hadn't. Ashen-faced, he turned abruptly away from her, picked up a grey pebble and hurled it into the sea. She watched him find another and then another, each time bigger stones, hurling them at the sea and swearing into the wind. Tears trickled down her face. That was it then. She started walking along the beach in the direction of home.

Eventually he caught her up. He had his hands in his pockets, coat collar turned up. 'What are you going to do?'

He was afraid. She saw it in his eyes.

'Dad's made an appointment. At the hospital. For a *termination*.' The word was loathsome, she thought. Like the other word. *Abortion*.

'When?'

'Thursday.'

'So you'll be all right then?'

'Yeah.'

'I'm sorry, Mia.'

'Yeah. Well.'

'What did your dad say?'

'What do you think? He went mad. He'd like to kill you.'

Will kept his distance the rest of the way. Didn't touch her once. She'd known he'd be like this. Shouldn't have told him. Should've kept her secret.

'Don't say anything, will you?' Mia's voice was cold. 'Don't tell anyone. Ever.'

'Don't they know already? Becky and Ali?'

'Just Becky. But she won't say anything. I can trust her.'

They walked further along the beach in silence.

Finally Will spoke again. 'It's not so terrible. Is it?'

Mia gritted her teeth. She mustn't cry. Not now. Not with him.

They'd reached the footpath and the turning to Mia's lane. Mia stopped. 'You can't come near the house. My dad really will kill you.'

She saw that look on his face again: fear, horror, a sort of blankness. Like Dad had looked when she'd told him.

'I'll be off then.' His words sounded strangled.

'OK.'

'See you around.'

'Yeah. Whatever.' Mia felt the ice freeze harder in her voice.

She watched his back as he trudged up the lane and took the turning to his house. He didn't look round. Was that it then? They would be like strangers to each other? She'd see him at school, larking about with Liam and Matt and people. Hanging around with Ali, no doubt. And they'd both know this horrible secret and neither would say anything about it?

She tried to imagine him going into his house, his mum calling out hello, him going upstairs to that room where she'd stayed the whole night in the bed with him without anyone knowing. He'd lie down on the bed, put on the headphones, let the music drown out his feelings until he had blanked it all out. So he could go downstairs into the kitchen and no one would guess what had happened. Life carried on.

Mia cried all the way up the road to her house. Then she made herself stop. As she turned the corner a car manoeuvred out of the drive. It looked vaguely familiar. Metallic grey, a Citroen or something.

Dad was standing at the sink rinsing out two mugs. Bags of shopping were stacked against the kitchen table. Mia pulled out a chair and slumped over the table. Dad stared at her. Her hand stroked her cropped head defensively.

'What on earth?' He stopped himself in his tracks. 'So that's where you've been. Hairdressers. That's a new one.' He paused, looking at her. 'Too short. But it suits you,' he added grudgingly. 'We had a visitor.'

Mia looked up. 'Who?'

'Your tutor.'

'What?! What does she want now?' Mia's voice was a knife blade.

'OK, calm down, it's no big deal. She called to see how things are. You weren't here. She had a cup of tea. That's all.'

Dad concentrated on wiping down the draining board. The back of his neck had gone red.

Who did he think she was? Naive or what? Scheming bitch. Trying to get her hands on her dad now. Using her as the excuse. That's all she needed. Dad going out with Miss Blackman. Imagine. Well she wasn't staying around for that. She'd find somewhere else to go.

'Oh, and Becky called by on her way home. To see how you are. Said she'll phone tonight. Sit down a minute, Mia. I want to talk to you about, you know, Thursday. I phoned your mother. Wait.'

Mia was halfway up the stairs.

'But she wasn't in. We'll try again later tonight.'

'I don't want her. I don't want to see her or any-one. Leave me alone, can't you?' Mia yelled down the stairs.

She slammed the bedroom door. The cat had been asleep on her bed. He raised his head, yawned so she could see his needle-sharp teeth and leathery tongue. For a moment he stared at her with big yellow eyes. Then he jumped off the bed and stalked towards the open window. She watched him. The tip of his ginger tail flicked as he watched the sparrows on the grass below, but it was too high to jump. He stretched out his legs and spread out his claws, then settled back for a nap on the window sill. He kept one ear alert, listening out for the birds, one eye half open, watching her.

Mia lay on the bed, hands over her belly.

'The baby is moving about gently to exercise its muscles, although you cannot feel these movements. At this point the baby weighs only about as much as a grape.'

Mia leaned over and slid the book back into the drawer under her bed.

A grape. A broad bean. Little bean. Sorry, sorry, sorry.

CHAPTER THIRTEEN

October 13th

'*Y*ou'll be all right then? I'll come back at lunchtime, and stay with you then. So I'll be here when you're having the anaesthetic, and everything – afterwards. Please let me phone your mum again.'

'No, Dad. I don't want her.'

Dad sighed heavily. 'Becky can come over, if you want. After school? Yes? I'm really sorry I can't wait with you all morning. But the nurse is lovely, isn't she? *Noreen*. You've got your book to read?'

'Yes, Dad. It's OK. Just go.'

He leaned over to give her a kiss, but she turned her head away and he just touched her hair instead.

She bit hard on her lip. No tears. She had the whole morning to get through now. They'd said she had to be here in Day Surgery at eight thirty, but then the ward nurse had come round and said she wasn't on the list till the afternoon. But she still had to get undressed and was supposed to lie on the bed, because the doctor would be round and he mustn't be kept waiting. So there was a whole morning to get through, and Dad had decided to go into work so he could take the afternoon off instead, and *be there for her.*

Mum had tried to talk to her on the phone Wednesday evening. Mia had listened to Dad's low tones, his quiet explanations. She could imagine Mum's shocked reaction on the other end. By the time she spoke to Mia, she sounded calm. 'Would you like me to come now? . . . Before? . . . You are sure about this, Mia? . . . I know I've no right to say anything about it. It's your decision. . . . You poor, poor thing.' But Mia hadn't wanted to talk. Said she didn't want her to come anyway. Dad was here, and Becky. She was all right.

For a brief second Mia wished she'd said, *Yes, please come. I need you. I'm scared and all by myself.*

But that wasn't true, was it? She was not *by herself* at all. Not yet. Not for a few hours longer. *Little bean.*

'All right, dear?' The nurse perched on the side of the bed, next to where Mia sat in the upright green chair.

'Is there anything you want to ask?'

Mia shook her head. Now she'd thought of little bean she couldn't speak. She bit back the tears. On her lap she held the sheaf of pages explaining how to relax and calm yourself down which Noreen had brought her earlier. Her hands were trembling.

The nurse put her hand over Mia's. 'I'm sorry, love. It's hard, isn't it? A bit scary?'

Tears welled up. Mia couldn't help it.

'I'll get you some tissues.'

Mia watched her walk between the rows of beds. In this half of the ward most of them were empty. There were a couple of older women in the beds near hers. They'd drawn the curtains round. One had a man with her, and the other, another woman. Her sister, maybe. That woman had asked the nurse where she could have a cigarette and the nurse had said she couldn't: 'Not till afterwards. If you must!'

The nurse came back with a box of tissues and left them on the bedside cabinet.

'The anaesthetist's arrived to do the ward round, love, so I have to go. Sorry I can't stay with you. I'll see you later. OK? What are you reading?'

Mia showed her the cover. *Tess of the D'Urbervilles*.

The nurse laughed. 'Bit heavy for me! I'm not brainy like you.'

'I'm not either. My dad gave it to me. Don't suppose I'll read it anyway.'

She put it back on the locker.

'Don't forget about getting your nightie on, love. And pop yourself on the bed. Doctor's round next.'

Mia didn't see what difference it made. All this scurrying around for the doctors. She wasn't getting undressed until the last minute. The minute you put on your night things you felt different. Sort of defenceless. She didn't own a *nightie*, anyway; she'd just brought a big T-shirt.

Mia's hands cupped protectively over her stomach. It was still flat. You'd never guess. Fleetingly she let herself wonder how long it would have been before it began to show. But some girls went for months, not knowing. Right up till the last minute. There were stories about it in the newspapers. Teenage girls thinking they had stomach cramp and the next minute they were giving birth.

Birth.

She wouldn't think about it.

Just a few cells. A blob, like Becky said.

Little bean.

No. No. Don't think. Watch the ward. Pick up the book. Footsteps. Look up . . .

The anaesthetist was a young man with an Australian accent. He smiled at Mia. He looked like he'd just stepped off a surfing beach, except for the white coat. He had undone it so it flapped open. He had blue shorts on underneath and tanned legs. He started to explain to her what would happen, and then he asked her a whole load of questions. 'Had she had an anaesthetic before? . . . Any allergic reactions?'

His voice was kind, like the nurse. Mia could feel the tears welling up again inside her.

'So I'll be looking after you all the time. But it's very quick. Only about five minutes and then it's all over.'

She stared at him. She'd been feeling so helpless and blank before, but now she felt something suddenly shift inside her. His words ran up and down her body and made her flesh prickle. *Then it's all over. All over.*

At the window a pigeon stared at her with its beady eye. It fluffed up its feathers and Mia saw how the grey was shot through with bright green, purple, silver. It spread out its wings, preened, shook and then took off. She could hear the wing beats, the whirr of feathers in flight.

'Are you all right? You are sure about this?' The anaesthetist sat down on the edge of the bed. He looked right at her. His eyes were very blue.

He spoke very quietly. So quietly, she wasn't sure

afterwards whether he'd actually said the words aloud at all. Perhaps they had been her words, inside her.

'You know you can change your mind at any moment? Even right up to the point where we wheel you in for the anaesthetic? It happens, you know. People do change their minds.'

Mia stared at him. The tears began to drip down her face again.

He patted her hand, and then he stood up and moved away, on to the next patient. She heard him talking to the woman behind the curtain. They laughed at some shared joke.

Mia watched him go back down the ward, his shoes squeaking softly on the lino. The pigeon was back on the window ledge. She heard it cooing gently. It preened its feathers for a while and then stared right in at her through the smeared window pane, cocked its head slightly as if to get a better look.

It's a sign. If it flies off it's a sign. The bird spread each wing, closed them again. Then it spread them again, launched off the ledge and flew up into the pale blue sky. *There!* She knew with sudden clarity what she must do.

The other beds still had the curtains drawn round. She stood up and tugged the horrible flowery curtains along the rail around her own bed. She found her washbag and T-shirt and purse in the locker, and stuffed them with her fleece jacket into the canvas bag she'd brought with her. She slipped her trainers back on. Then she looked at the time. Nine thirty-five.

The nurse, Noreen, was in the other half of the ward, getting the first people ready for theatre. 'It's a mixed ward for day surgery,' she'd told Mia. 'Everyone's here for different operations. No one will know what you're here for.' Between the two halves of the big airy ward were the loos, and the double doors into the hospital corridor. Easy. If Noreen saw her she'd assume she was going to the loo.

But Noreen didn't even notice her. Mia walked quietly past the curtained beds, out into the lobby and then through the double doors into the corridor. She kept walking down the long corridor, past the sets of doors opening off on either side, making straight for the exit. It only took a few minutes. Then she pushed the door open and she was outside in the pale sunshine of the hospital car park. She kept going. Across the car park, down the road, through the big gates on to the main road. Free.

CHAPTER FOURTEEN

The hospital was a mile or two from the town centre.
Better catch a bus. Then she'd be back in Ashton well
before Dad left work.

She felt light-headed with relief, walking along
the busy street away from the hospital, her bag over
her shoulder. They'd forced her into it really, hadn't
they? But she could choose. Why should she do what
they wanted? Didn't she always do that? Well, not
now, not any more. She'd show them. Why shouldn't
she be a mother? What did age have to do with it?
She'd find a way.

Mia sat on the top floor of the bus at the front.
She'd not been along this route before. The bus didn't
go straight into town like she'd expected, but turned
off and meandered through huge estates of houses
she didn't know existed. At each stop there were
groups of mothers with small kids and pushchairs.

Mia stared out of the window at the rows of terraced houses, the semis with paired front gardens, neat squares with clipped rose trees next to wild wastelands of bindweed and dandelion, rusting swings and half-dismantled motorbikes. On the outskirts of Ashton the bus lurched along a pot-holed road to a row of houses near the old gas works.

Mia's heart skipped a beat – a small girl was sitting on the low wall in front of one of the houses. Lainey? The bus had gone past the stop, but Mia was sure it had been her. She craned back to get another glimpse. The child had turned too, gazing back at Mia. She saw Lainey's dark eyes, her halo of fair hair, the thin cotton dress she'd worn that first time Mia'd seen her on the bridge. Impulsively, Mia pressed the bell. The bus driver swore, braked, barked something at Mia as she clattered down the stairs and out of the door. She didn't care.

The figure had disappeared from the wall. Now Mia couldn't be sure on which wall exactly she had seen Lainey; the walls and houses all looked exactly the same. She hovered on the pavement, suddenly uncomfortable. A woman stared at her through one of the windows opposite. Now she could hear a baby crying. Perhaps it was Lainey's baby, the baby who was sick. But there was no sign of Lainey. What was she playing at? She'd definitely seen Mia, the way she'd turned and watched the bus. But maybe she hadn't realized Mia would get off the bus to find her. Should she knock on one of the doors now she was here? If only the woman didn't look so hostile, standing there watching her.

A car careered past, splashing right through a puddle and drenching Mia's legs. Two youths hung out of the windows and laughed. The woman at the window turned her back on Mia. In the house next door someone was playing music. A light was on upstairs. She'd nothing to lose, had she? She'd knock on the door and ask which house was Lainey's. She had to find her, tell her what had happened. About her baby.

Baby Baby Baby. She said the word over and over in her head, trying to take it in, make it real. She, Mia, with a baby! And then the thought came, Lainey would be pleased. Lainey would understand.

The rain started again while Mia wondered whether she dared knock. The door suddenly opened and a man with grey hair tied back in a ponytail looked directly at her.

'Do you want something?'

Mia nodded. 'Does a little girl, Lainey, live here? One of these houses?'

He shrugged. 'Not here. Dunno. Millions of kids round here. What's she look like?'

'Little. Thin. About eight. She was out on the street just a minute ago. Fair hair, sort of fluffed up round her head. In an old-fashioned sort of summer dress?'

He shrugged again. 'Can't help you. Sorry.'

She knew he was watching her as she walked along the pavement. Creepy. She wished she'd stayed on the bus. Her bag was heavy, dragging at her shoulder. Now she'd have to walk into town and where was she going to go then? Dad would be making his way to the hospital any minute. They must have realized she'd gone missing; there'd be police called out or something.

What on earth was she going to do?

Mia turned away from the gas works and walked back to the main road. Too bad if they saw her. Where did she think she was going to hide anyway? They'd catch up with her sooner or later.

The main road was busy with traffic. The narrow pavement petered out altogether once she'd got past the refuse depot and she had to huddle into the edge of the buildings that lined this section of the road. Water sprayed up from the puddles as cars splashed by. Her trainers were already soaked. How did Lainey manage this busy road? Or did her mother drop her off somewhere in town each morning, thinking she was going into school?

At last she reached the part of Ashton she recognized. Factories and warehouses changed to office blocks, car parks, the college where Becky wanted to do her textiles course next year. Then the first row of shops. Mia headed for the old market. So far, so good. No one had stopped her. No police-car sirens. No sign of Dad.

Mia ordered herself a hot chocolate in the market cafe. Her feet were freezing in the sodden trainers. Her hands shook as she took the mug from the counter.

'You OK, love?'

Mia nodded. Mustn't cry.

'Look. You sit down and I'll bring it over. You can't carry it like that! The world on your shoulders! What you got in there? The kitchen sink?'

Mia squeezed herself along the row of plastic chairs fixed to the floor alongside the table in the far corner of the cafe.

'There you are, love. You're wet through, aren't you?'

Mia fumbled in her bag for her purse. She hoped the woman hadn't seen inside her bag. All her stuff. She mustn't look suspicious.

'I've seen you in here before, haven't I?' The woman wanted to chat.

'Yes.'

Mia didn't want to talk. But then she remembered the last time she'd been here, with Lainey. Perhaps this woman knew Lainey too? She might be able to help.

'I come in here with a little girl sometimes. Thin, fair hair, wears funny sort of clothes? Have you seen her?'

'Can't say I remember her. But we get all sorts here. It's cheap and cheerful, isn't it? Not those silly prices you pay in the posh places.'

Two people were queuing at the counter; the woman had to go back to serve them. Mia warmed her hands on the mug of hot chocolate and planned her next move. The river. If Lainey wasn't there, she'd give up and go home.

Home? How could she possibly go there now? What could she possibly say to Dad? He'd go completely mental. He'd probably kill her. And then Will. The enormity of what she'd done began to trickle through.

All the recent rain had swelled the river, churned it brown and swirling and fast. Not much more and it would burst the banks. The water raced under the bridge, thick and dark. Whole trees were being whirled downstream. Further down the river a shabby, patched-up narrow boat was moored; the sort you live in, with a wood-burning stove and curtains at the little windows. There was smoke coming from a chimney. Mia watched a woman on the deck unpacking a bike pannier, and then a younger woman appeared on deck and waved up at the bridge. Mia turned to see who she was waving at.

She gasped. There she was again, perched on the parapet like a bird about to take flight, her hair lifting in the wind. Lainey, bird-child, looking as if she might fall at any moment. Mia rushed back towards the steps, but Lainey was safely back on the road already, her pointed little face beaming at Mia. 'There you are! Good. I knew you'd come.'

'What do you mean? And how –'

'How's your baby then?'

Mia flushed. 'I'm going to keep the baby after all. I wanted to tell you, Lainey. I knew you'd be glad. I've just come from the hospital. I changed my mind. Ran away. Just now. This morning. And I wanted to tell you.'

'Good. We'll both have babies then, won't we? My baby's getting better.'

'I thought I saw you, earlier. At your house. Didn't you see me, on the bus? I got off specially.'

Lainey just laughed. She waved again at the girl on the boat. 'See them? You know, from that stall? I told them about you, but they'd already spotted you. They're kind. They give me dinner sometimes. Are you hungry? Come on. You can meet them.'

Lainey skipped along the river path; Mia panted behind, out of breath, trying to keep up.

'Why do you do that, Lainey? Go up on the bridge like you were a moment ago? It isn't safe, you know. And I'm sure it was you back on the estate. You saw me, didn't you? On that bus? Where did you go?'

'Don't you ever stop asking stuff? It makes my head hurt.'

They'd reached the moored boat. Mia could read its name now, painted in blue along the peeling green side: *Dragonfly*. The dark-haired woman smiled at them both. Mia recognized her now. She had that stall by the wall in the precinct, with the 'Temporary Tattoos' sign, where she laid out hair braids and Indian-looking stuff, embroidered wrist bands and necklaces made of glittery beads, beautiful bags. Too expensive for Mia.

'This is Mia,' Lainey said. 'She's my friend. Can we come on the boat?'

Mia ignored the voice in her head. Dad's voice, drummed into her over years and years, warning her to '*be careful, beware strangers*'. Walking out of the hospital ward, she'd stepped over some invisible line. Now anything was possible.

The woman held out her hand to steady Mia as she stepped across from the slippery bank.

'Evie,' she introduced herself. 'Hello. And that's Shannon.'

Mia had seen her before too: that amazing head of auburn hair braided into masses of tiny plaits, the bright orange mohair jumper. She was skinny, like Mia. Dark eyes. She didn't look much older than Mia.

'Hi. We've seen you around. Wondered about you. Thought you might be one of us. Your hair's different, isn't it? Not long enough for braids now. Suits you!' Shannon smiled.

One of us? What did she mean?

'You're soaked. Want to come in out of the rain for a bit?' Evie asked.

Mia looked towards Lainey.

'It's fine. You go. I'm busy. Bye.'

'Hang on, Lainey! Wait! Where are you going?' But Lainey was already skipping back along the path towards the bridge. Mia stood there, stranded. Embarrassed.

'Well? You coming in or not?' Evie smiled warmly at Mia.

'Sorry. OK. Thanks.'

What else could she do? It was pouring with rain. She had nowhere else to go.

She followed Evie through the wooden door of the narrow boat, down the step into the cabin.

Inside, it was dark and smelled strange. Incense? Oils? Mia wrinkled up her nose. The small windows were draped with swathes of embroidered and sequinned cloth, like the quilt on the low beds which lined the narrow space. Deep reds and purples and gold. At the far end there was a little kitchen, with a wood burner and even a tiny sink and draining board. There were shelves above it, and mugs on hooks. Like a play house. Becky would love it.

'Sit down then. Take off your wet things. Shannon's making soup. Want some? You look frozen.'

'Thanks. If it's OK? I'm starving.'

Mia took off her wet fleece. She shivered. She was chilled through. She watched Evie ladle out three bowls. She hadn't eaten anything since last night, she realized. You weren't allowed to eat anything after twelve the night before the operation, because of the anaesthetic.

The soup tasted wonderful. Evie nodded at Mia's empty soup bowl. 'You needed that. How come you were so hungry? What've you been doing?'

Mia hunched on the edge of the seat, suddenly shy again. 'Well –'

'Stop hassling, Evie. Give her some space,' Shannon interrupted.

Evie looked crushed. She ladled some more soup into Mia's bowl, and they ate in silence. The rain battered against the roof.

Finally Mia looked up. 'So do you both live here? On the boat?'

'Yes,' Evie said. 'Lovely, isn't it?'

'Better in the summer, when it's not always raining,' Shannon said. 'But it's cool. Beats houses. We can just move on whenever we need to!'

'What did you mean,' Mia asked, 'when you said I was *one of us*?'

'What?'

'When I first got here, you said you thought I might be *one of us*.'

Shannon smiled. 'Oh, that! Nothing much. You know, bunking off school, doing your own thing. A free spirit. Like us. We've seen you around lately. That's all.'

It was odd to think she'd been noticed. She'd thought of herself as invisible, wandering round Ashton alone these last weeks. 'I've seen you before too. Your stall. With all the Indian stuff,' Mia said. 'My friend Becky loves all that stuff. She'd love this too.' Mia stroked the embroidered quilt on the couch. Thinking of Becky made her feel suddenly lonely.

'So,' Evie leaned forward eagerly, 'let me guess your story. Everyone has a story, you know.'

'Evie? Shut it. Can't you see she's all done in?'

Sooner or later she'd have to tell them. What she'd done. About the baby. Right now, all she wanted to do was sleep.

Squalls of rain battered the windows, like gravel against glass. The boat bumped against the bank, tugging at the mooring rope. The river made a roaring sound, rushing down towards the weir.

They sat with her for hours, it seemed, while she dozed. Waited, patiently. Every so often, Evie opened a can of beer, or lit a cigarette. Shannon flicked through a magazine.

Now Mia was properly awake, Evie leaned forward again.

'So what's your story, Mia? Parents? Boyfriend? Beating you up or something? Or school?'

Shannon got up from her seat next to the stove. 'Don't let her go on at you, Mia. You don't have to tell us anything if you don't want to.'

'It's all right. I don't mind. I want to tell you. I haven't told anyone yet. Except Lainey.'

Evie opened another can of beer.

Mia's mouth felt dry. She looked down at her feet as she talked, mumbling her words. 'This morning. I was at the hospital. For an operation. But I couldn't let them do it. Now I don't know what to do.'

She began to cry.

Evie glanced towards Shannon. 'It's OK. An abortion, right?'

'But I couldn't – I really couldn't – and so I ran out – and where do I go now? What on earth am I going to do?'

Evie sipped at the can. She offered some to Mia, who shook her head. 'It'll make me sick.'

'So you're pregnant. That's not so bad, you know. It's just what *they* tell you. Some people would be pleased.' Evie looked at Shannon, who said nothing. 'So go on then. You might as well tell us the rest.'

She told them everything. About Dad. Will, little bean.

Evie and Shannon listened, and nodded, and drank more beer.

'Well,' Evie finally said. 'It's hard. But you'll be OK. You've got us now. Running away, moving on: that's what we do best, isn't it, Shannon?'

'Cool it, Evie. She's just a kid.'

Mia flushed. 'You don't look much older than me.'

'How old are you?'

'Fifteen. Nearly sixteen.'

'How nearly?' Evie asked.

'February.'

'And your baby will be born when?'

Mia felt confused again. 'I – well – I suppose May.'

'You're going to have it then?' Shannon asked.

'Well, yes. At the hospital, this morning, I suddenly just sort of knew. I couldn't let them do that to me. And the baby.'

Shannon nodded. 'Good. That's cool. You'll be a great mother. Won't she, Evie?'

But Evie didn't answer. She bent forward to pick up the empty beer cans, so her hair hid her face, and then carried them into the kitchen area and started riddling the stove noisily. Mia looked at Shannon for some sort of explanation, but her face was blank, watching Evie.

Shannon turned back towards Mia. 'So what do you want to do now?'

'I haven't thought. I don't know. They'll be looking for me by now. I suppose I have to let Dad know I'm OK.'

Shannon nodded.

'But if I go back home, they'll try to make me –' Mia started to cry again. 'I don't want to go back there.'

'It's OK. You don't have to go anywhere. You and your baby.' Evie had regained her composure. She came right over to Mia and put an arm round her shoulders. 'Don't worry. We'll help you.'

Her sudden warmth made Mia cry more. She'd walked out of that hospital ward this morning expecting nothing but criticism, rejection. And yet here she was, a few hours later, on a strange boat, being comforted by two women who knew nothing about her really. Were completely different from her, far removed from her life in Whitecross. But they weren't cross. Didn't judge. Had welcomed her with open arms.

Shannon lit the candle lantern in the kitchen area and it threw shadows around the cramped space.

When Mia finally stopped crying, Shannon spoke gently to her. 'So how come you've not mentioned your mum so far, Mia? Where's she?'

'Bristol, now. She left us when I was little. Dad, and my sisters and me,' Mia began to explain.

The shadows stretched and quivered, and the narrow boat bumped and bobbed on the swollen river. For the first time in ages, Mia felt she wasn't alone.

CHAPTER FIFTEEN

*M*ia slept. Darkness gathered around her, seeping in from the corners of the narrow boat and settling like a blanket over her. And her dreams were full of muddle and pain. She woke at last, sweating and anxious. Evie and Shannon still sat there, watching her. The boat smelled stuffy, a sweet smell she didn't recognize.

Evie leaned over her. 'Awake? It's getting late.'

Mia felt dazed. 'What time is it?'

'Nearly seven. Look, Mia. You have to tell your dad you're all right or else he'll come searching for you and there'll be police and all that,' Shannon said.

'I'll go with you, if you want. Need to get some food for tonight. The Spar will still be open.' Evie started getting her coat on, lacing her boots.

Mia cowered back on the low cushions, her stomach churning with fear. This would really be it, this time. It would be like the time she was done for trying to buy cider at the off-licence, only much, much worse. Shouting and threats and she'd be dragged off home to Whitecross or maybe the social worker people would say she had to go into care or something.

'Leave your bag here,' Shannon said. 'You can't go round carrying that all the time. I'll look after it. Promise.' She smiled. 'You're scared now, but you'll feel better when you've told your dad you're staying with us.'

'Am I?' Mia looked nervously at Evie, and then back to Shannon. 'Is it OK?'

'Well, where else are you going to go? Course it's OK.'

Mia fished a couple of twenty-pence pieces from her purse.

She pressed the numbers with numb fingers. Her heart thumped as she listened to the phone ringing, then the click as it was snatched up.

'Mia?'

'Yes.'

'Where the hell are you? I've been worried sick.'

'Wait – listen –'

'You've gone one step too far this time. What do you think you're playing at? Can you *imagine* the scene at the hospital – and when I turned up – but no, it's not possible for you to imagine anything, is it, apart from your stupid fantasies of doing what you want regardless of anyone else.'

Mia held the phone away from her ear. She turned to Evie who was waiting a few feet away, but her back was turned. Inside the booth it smelled of stale urine and fags. Mia thought she'd vomit any minute. Dad's voice yelled on and on. She closed her eyes. Waves of nausea washed through her. She gripped the receiver more tightly.

'Dad, *listen*. I'm OK, I'm staying with some people – just people, OK? I'm not telling you who. I'll phone tomorrow when you've calmed down. *Shut up!* I had to get out of the hospital. I changed my mind. Listen! Well, I'd never made it up in the first place, but in there I did. I worked it out. That I don't want to get rid of it, like all the rest of you.'

He wouldn't listen. Mia banged the receiver back, pushed the heavy door open and retched in the gutter.

Evie wandered over and put a hand on her back. Mia shrugged it off. She didn't want anyone to touch her. No one. Not ever again. Close up, Evie smelled disgusting, a mix of stale cigarette smoke and alcohol.

'Ready? Coming back?' Evie turned towards the river.

Mia followed. It was beginning to rain again. She let the tears run down her cheeks unchecked.

'How much money have you got?' Evie asked her. 'We need something for supper. The soup's all finished already.'

'Sorry.'

'Don't be daft. That's what it was for. Anyway, you need to eat. You look starved. Thin as an alley cat. That baby of yours, eating it all up, I suppose. Or do you always look like that?'

Mia shrugged. 'Dunno. Like this, I s'pose. Dad goes on about it sometimes. And the hospital.' She glanced at Evie. It was impossible to guess whether she was thin or fat or whatever, under her layers and layers of clothes – bright webby wool jumpers and Indian cotton skirts and leggings and now a thick man's overcoat wound round with a velvet scarf. She was probably quite small and thin really. Her face was, under the braided dreadlocks and purple head band.

Mia took a five pound note from her purse. She didn't have much left now, what with the bus fare, and the cafe. But if Evie and Shannon were letting her stay, it seemed right to give over the money and help get some food. She huddled behind Evie as she shopped in the supermarket for vegetables and tins of tomatoes and bread, head down, praying that no one would recognize her.

'We'll have soup again,' Evie said. 'It's cheap, and good for you, and you can cook it all in one pan, which makes life easier on the boat. And we'll have to get some coke for the stove on the way back. Joe on the canal sells it. We'll go back that way.'

'Where d'you get your money from?' Mia asked.

'Here and there. Selling stuff. The stall. Every so often we do a trip, somewhere like India, bring back a load of stuff to sell. That's where I first met Shannon, India. People pay good money for cushion covers and hats and bags and stuff when it's the real thing. Mirrors, embroidery, silk. You've seen our stall, haven't you? Sometimes we sign on, if we're staying in one place. But mostly we like to keep moving. We've been in this dump long enough, only Shannon's got a thing about this bloke – Joe. And it's easy to get a mooring here. But we'll need to move on soon. We haven't got much stuff left to sell. We need another trip to India, only we haven't got enough money for that.'

'Where else d'you go then?'

'Anywhere. By water. There's a whole network of rivers and canals – some of them no good any more. But you can get all the way to London if you want. Then again, why would anyone want to do that? It's better out of the cities really. Unless you're wanting to hide.'

Mia hung back while Evie haggled with Joe over the coke. Joe smoothed back his long black hair with a coal-stained hand as he talked. Evie finally handed over a wodge of notes, and Joe hugged her before disappearing back into his boat. There were loads of boats, moored up next to each other, all different kinds and sizes, and most of them shabby and patched. They had names like *Freedom*, *Wanderlust*, *Romany Star*. Joe's boat was smarter than most of the others. It looked newly painted. Bright blue. *Kingfisher*. Smoke curled up from the chimney; there were pots of herbs and flowers on the top. And piles of yellow bags of coal. Several of the boats had generators whirring round. Lean dogs nosed along the grass at the edge of the towpath. Someone had cleared a patch at the side of the path and made a rough wooden bench, and there was a swing tied to a bough of the tree hanging over the rough ground. An old pram, a child's bike, a pot of faded geraniums. A whole parallel world, a stone's throw from the drab streets and shops and houses of the town.

They walked back along the towpath towards the river. Mia helped carry the bag of coke. The rain soaked through her fleece and her trainers squelched through puddles and mud on the path. Her hands were numb with cold by the time they got back.

The boat was in darkness. No sign of Shannon. No smoke from the stove. It smelled of damp river water, cold. Mia wondered how she'd ever get warm again. Back home, Dad would be slumped over the kitchen table, or maybe stretched out in the sitting room with the telly on and a glass of beer. Or maybe Miss Blackman would have rallied to his support, and she'd be there too, offering comfort. Mia felt sick again. She thought of Kate, somewhere in France, or probably Italy by now, sitting in sunshine surrounded by new and exciting friends. Laura, back at Bristol, in those boring halls of residence, but warm and dry and happy in her own way. Becky. Her mum chatting with her while they cooked a family supper. Will, lying on his bed listening to music, or practising his sax, or – she was crying properly now, full of self-pity – phoning some girl, Ali probably, on his mobile.

'Get the stove going. The stuff's all there.'

Evie was talking to her. But she didn't have a clue how to light the stove. She was too cold and wet and miserable to do anything.

'Get a move on. Stop feeling sorry for yourself and help. If you're staying here you have to muck in, you know. Pregnant or not.'

Mia fumbled with kindling wood and coke. She tried to remember the way Dad made fires, like they'd had years ago at Christmas. He rolled newspaper into sticks, coiled them round into snakes, placed these among wood and sticks, but maybe a stove was different?

'For heaven's sake! Can't you even make a fire?' Evie shoved her aside. 'Watch, then you can do it next time.'

Through tear-filled eyes, Mia watched the little curl of flame lick along the kindling sticks and turn from yellow to blue as she added the coke. Smoke started to billow out and Evie shut the glass door on the front of the stove.

'There. Keep an eye on it. You control the draught with the little knob underneath, see? And it will need feeding with coke. A fire's like a living thing. Now, can you cook?'

Mia sniffed. 'A bit. I can chop stuff if you like, for the soup.'

Her hands were still freezing. And her feet wet.

'I'm sorry, Evie. But can I borrow some socks or something, and a jumper?'

'Course! You're soaked, aren't you? I'll find you something.' She rummaged in a black bin bag under the seat at the back of the boat and pulled out a collection of jumpers, socks, leggings.

Swaddled in strange clothes, Mia huddled next to the stove and chopped leeks and carrots for soup. Rain clattered on the roof of the boat. Mia felt the boat tugging and chafing against the mooring ropes; it wanted to go with the river current, rushing towards the estuary. The two thin ropes were all that kept them safe. She thought of the cold dark depth running underneath them. If you fell in, you would be swept and swirled downstream before anyone heard your cry for help. She shivered.

Mia slept fitfully on the mattress, blankets piled over her clothed body. She woke once to hear voices. Evie and Shannon were arguing about something. A third voice joined in; Mia opened her eyes and saw Joe from the canal standing next to the stove, rolling a cigarette. She closed her eyes again and let the voices drift over her. Later she heard Evie again, fragments of conversation: 'We could take her . . . it'd be cool . . . canal . . . Bristol . . . mother . . . a baby.'

They must be talking about her. She tried to listen, but Shannon had noticed she was awake and shushed Evie, who was saying something about a baby. Mia drifted back to sleep, and when she next awoke the boat was in darkness. She could just make out Evie's shape under the covers on the opposite mattress. Shannon and Joe had disappeared. Back to his boat, presumably.

The boat bumped and buffeted the bank. The rain still fell. Mia hugged her arms around her own body and wished that she was at home and that it was the beginning of the summer, before everything had gone so badly wrong.

CHAPTER SIXTEEN

October 14th

*W*hen Mia woke up it was still dark in the boat; very little light filtered through the drapes over the small windows. Rain was still drumming on the roof. Mia watched Evie open the stove and add more fuel. She placed a pan of water on the blackened top for tea, and started rolling a cigarette.

I shouldn't be breathing this in, all this smoke. It's bad for the baby. She felt nauseous again, like she always did first thing. The smell of smoke made it worse. Her body ached from lying all night hunched up under the thin covers trying to keep herself warm. She'd have to find somewhere else to go. Somewhere where there was proper light and heat, for a start.

That half-heard fragment of conversation from the night before, the mention of *Bristol* and *mother* – perhaps that wasn't such a bad idea. She wasn't going home anyway. She couldn't bear the thought of being alone with Dad, and Miss Blackman's visits, and everyone in the village noticing her swelling belly and the tongues all wagging – *I told you so* – that woman up the lane nosy-parkering her way in.

But Mum? She wouldn't want Mia around, not now she was starting off in her new house with her new man and her job and everything, and Mia wouldn't know anyone else in Bristol apart from Laura, who definitely wouldn't want her spoiling things. And how on earth was she going to manage for money? She'd have to get some job or something, but how could she do that when the baby came? How was she going to look after a baby night and day anyway?

She must have been mad, yesterday, thinking she could do it all by herself. Dad was right. She was living in a sort of fantasy where everything would somehow be all right, and money would just appear like magic. She'd have this beautiful little baby who would love her forever and ever and they'd grow up like sisters or best friends. *Sometimes it turns out OK, of course. Once in a blue moon. But mostly it doesn't. You have to face the truth, Mia.*

'You're awake then.'

'Yes.'

'You look a bit green. You going to throw up?'

Mia shook her head.

'There's a bucket out there.' Evie gestured towards the doors on to the deck.

Perhaps she'd feel better in the fresh air. Mia stumbled towards the doors and turned the handle. The wind snatched the door and swung it wide and Mia heard Evie cursing her.

She did feel better outside, even though the air was damp and cold. The river ran swift and deep, tugging the boat and swirling old bits of branch and rubbish down towards the weir. On the towpath a man cycled slowly along, dodging the large muddy puddles. He raised a hand to Mia. Must think she was someone else. Mia shivered. She was hungry now. Longed for warmth; her own bed, a shower. She went back into the boat.

Evie had made tea. Mia cupped her hands round the mug and sipped at the sour mixture.

'It's chamomile. Soothing. Toast?'

Evie held chunks of bread on the end of a fork in front of the open stove and Mia watched the edges brown in the light from the flames. It tasted good. The boat began to warm up.

'You'd better go and get some of your clothes and stuff.' Evie was matter of fact. 'Then we can get going.'

'What do you mean?'

'Me and Shannon. We decided we'll take you all

the way on the boat to your mum's place you told us about. Joe's got a map. We can do the whole distance by river and canal. Time we were moving on anyway. We might as well go there as any place else.'

'To Bristol? From here? In this? How long will that take?'

'You're not in a hurry, are you? Be there well before May, in any case. Give your mum time to get used to the idea of a baby.'

Mia curled up on the mattress. The lump of panic in her belly settled rock hard. Evie was waiting for her to say something.

'Well, I'm not sure. I don't really know if that's a good idea. I mean, my mum – I haven't seen her for ages.'

'She's still your mum, though, isn't she?'

'Yes – but – well, she left us, didn't she? That's the whole point. She didn't want us. She wanted a new life. She couldn't stand us children any more.'

'Don't be daft. It wasn't anything to do with you. It was your dad and her. Their stuff. Anyway, you're not a child any more, are you? And where else can you go? You got a better idea?'

'No, well, not yet. It's too sudden.'

'They'll come looking for you soon, and we don't want any hassle, so get your stuff if you're coming. We'll get the boat ready today and go tomorrow morning. Providing Shannon can prise herself away from Joe, of course. We'll have to get on to the canal first, up through the locks. That'll take a morning or so, but Joe will be around to help. You won't be much good on the lock gates. They're too heavy.'

Evie was right. There didn't seem to be any option really. She should be grateful that she'd landed on her feet so easily; found people to help her. She should stop being so scared and muddled. Get her stuff. Thank her lucky stars.

After breakfast, Mia counted out her money. Enough for the bus home and back. Then she'd have to find some more. Dad might have left some behind the clock, if she was lucky. She'd have to trust that he'd gone to work as usual. Wouldn't think what would happen if he was waiting there for her, or her mother, or Becky or someone from school.

She timed it carefully. No one she knew was on the bus; Whitecross was deserted. A few cars passed her as she walked along the main road from the village and then up the lane, but no one stopped. No cars in the drive.

The house was empty. No police guard or spying social workers or anything. Not even a note from Dad in case she turned up. He'd tidied up. There was washing in the machine, on the final spin. Odd.

Like walking into someone else's house: she was a stranger here already. Everything carrying on without her. Easier for everyone if she wasn't there.

Mia found a rucksack in the cupboard under the stairs, took it with her up to her room, bundled in some clean clothes. She stood for a moment looking out of the bedroom window. The leaves of the ash tree had all fallen, wiped off by the rain and wind that had lashed the house all night. Her room seemed small, childish. The photographs on the chest of drawers smiled weakly back at her. She picked up the old one of her mum, scrutinized the face for a moment as if looking for a sign, some sort of encouragement.

Just as she was leaving the room she noticed the old pregnancy book lying on the floor by the bed and picked it up, shoved it into the rucksack with the clothes. Then she remembered her notebook and a pen in the top drawer of the bedside cabinet and she put them in too. Downstairs, she rummaged behind the clock. There were three twenty-pound notes. Good. On the top of the usual stack of letters was a new one, mum's writing on the envelope. Addressed to her. Mia put it in the bag to read later. No time to waste now. She pulled the front door shut and walked back through the damp garden to the gate. The cat was crouched under the tree, watching her with his slit eyes as if even he didn't recognize her. No place for her here, she could see now. No choice left but to go.

There wouldn't be a bus for ages. Mia walked down the lane, then took the muddy footpath to the shore. She went past the field, Will's and her field, where everything had started to go wrong. You'd never guess; just some old empty field with grass and mud. She crunched across the stones on the beach and then took off the rucksack, went empty-handed to the edge of the water. The sea was quite high, covering the mud and stones and weed that would lie stinking and ugly when the tide went out. There was hardly any wind now; it had blown itself out after the wild night. The small waves limped in, folded over each other with a gentle shooshing sound. Her eyes travelled over the bay, to the hills the other side. She could just make them out through the mist. Mia closed her eyes and let the sound of the water soothe her. *Don't think. No need here. Just the sounds. Listen.*

She remembered coming down to this beach one Christmas Eve with Dad and Kate and Laura. They gathered up driftwood and Dad built a fire. '*Better than fairylights*,' Dad said, and Mia watched the tiny glowing sparks rush out of the fire into the dark sky and then float down on to the pebbles. '*Magic*,' he said. *'They're real fairies,'* and Mia had believed him. She must have been seven or eight.

'Clap hands all the children who believe in fairies.' That was at *Peter Pan*, in the old theatre at Ashton that wasn't there any more, and they had all clapped to save Tinkerbell, even though Mia didn't really believe any more. How old was she then? Nine or ten? Even her sisters had clapped their hands. But not Dad.

A seagull swooped in on long white wings and settled back on the water near Mia. It folded the wings back over its body, so the tips crossed into the tail. Will would have known exactly what kind of gull it was.

For some reason the gull made her think of Lainey. Perhaps she'd turn up at the river again today. Mia hoped she would. Wouldn't it be nice if Lainey could come too on the boat? She wondered what Lainey's story really was. What had happened to her, that she slipped in and out of the town unnoticed, in and out of other lives, and no one took care of her, saw that she had warm clothes and food? Was Mia, too, slipping over the edge into that separate world, the parallel one, along with the boat people on the canal with their thin dogs, or the young people you saw crouched on the pavements in the town, mumbling requests for money for something to eat, for a ticket to get home, for fags, for booze, for a place to sleep?

Mia heaved the rucksack over one shoulder and walked slowly along the deserted beach in the direction of the village. If she timed it right, she wouldn't have to wait too long at the bus stop. She could slip away from Whitecross unnoticed.

On the bus, Mia remembered the letter from Mum and pulled it out of her bag. She read it quickly, then again, more slowly, trying to take it in, feeling her anger rise with each sentence.

I keep thinking about you. I feel terrible. Why do you cut me out of your life like this? I would have come to be with you, but you reject every move I make, don't you? I know it must have been awful for you, getting pregnant, although I still can't believe you'd be so foolish. Well, you've learned the hardest way.

It's a horrible thing to have to go through, an abortion, but having a baby at your age would have been even worse. At least your father was right about that. The sheer exhaustion of looking after another human being twenty-four hours a day, never getting enough sleep, never being able to go out by yourself – it's hard enough when you're older and have money coming into the household. So I'm sure you'll come to see it was the best thing in the circumstances. At least this way you can carry on with school and get your exams under your belt. Then you can decide what you want to do next, really find your wings and fly. The whole world's out there, Mia. It's taken me a long, long time to find it. I feel I'm only just taking off now at my grand old age! But it will be different for you. You won't be tied down like I was.

Mia scrumpled up the letter and held it so tight her knuckles went white. Her whole body trembled with rage. How dare she? What kind of a mother said things like that? How could she possibly go and see her now?

At Ashton bus station, Mia followed the line of shoppers into the dreary precinct. It was only eleven thirty. The whole day stretched out before her. She couldn't face going back to the boat yet. She'd have to tell Evie and Shannon about the letter. Mia went along to the market instead and ordered a hot chocolate and toast. It wasn't very busy, and the usual woman wasn't there. A man served her at the counter and watched her as she settled herself at a table near the wall. Then he buried himself in his newspaper again. Her head felt fuzzy; she was tired out. She gazed into space for a while and then rummaged in the rucksack for the pregnancy book.

*

'*Week 11 ... the sickness should gradually lessen from now onwards. The amount of blood circulating through your body has started to increase ... You should be thinking about arranging antenatal classes. Your baby's testicles or ovaries have formed, as have all of its major organs.*'

A boy, or a girl. It was already decided. Little bean, growing week by week inside her. It was unimaginable.

She put the book away and opened the notebook instead. She doodled with the pen, spirals and circles. It made her think of school. Taking notes. Will. *I'll have to tell him that I'm keeping the baby. He's got a right to know. He'll be a father, and nothing can change that. My baby's father. And his mum and dad will be grandparents. Like my mum and dad. Whether I like it or not.*

Evie looked up from the boat deck as Mia came along the path by the river.

'You're back then? We'd almost given up. Thought you'd chickened out. Got your stuff OK then?'

'Yes. No one at home.'

Mia balanced along the plank and Evie held out a hand to steady her.

'It's cold. I was just going back in.' Evie opened the boat doors and Mia followed her. She dumped the rucksack in the corner. Evie nodded. 'I'll find you a place for your stuff, OK? You'll have to keep tidy on the boat. Not much space. So, we'll leave in the morning then. The river's high. All that rain. It'll be better on the canal anyway. Safer. It might just be you and me to begin with.' Evie looked pained. 'Shannon wants to come on later with Joe. Stupid girl. It's not good for her, hanging around him.'

'Evie?' Mia hesitated, not sure how to go on. 'I'm not sure, Evie. I don't think my mum's going to want me. I don't want to go to her really.'

Evie rattled the bucket of coal she was shovelling into the stove. Her voice was suddenly thick with irritation. 'Make your mind up. I'm going anyway. Take it or leave it. You'll have to find somewhere else to go though. Back to your dad? Is that what you want?' She put down the coal bucket and reached down a drink can from the shelf. She couldn't pull the ring to open it with her mittened fingers, threw off the mittens, tried again. She gulped the beer, not looking at Mia.

'I'm going out. Make up your mind, right? By the time I get back. And don't let the stove go out.'

Mia sat hunched in the boat. Through the little window she watched Evie wheel her bike down the plank and then ride away down the towpath. She felt cold even wrapped up in her thickest jumper and with Evie's old woollen socks pulled up over her own. It was as if the cold of the water deep below had permeated the boat, her clothes, everything. The boat was tugging and swinging round like it had done in the night, the brown water swirling and eddying round. She hoped Evie had tied the rope properly. She seemed unfriendly, hostile even. Impatient with Mia's indecisiveness. Just like Dad. With Dad though it was different. He knew her really well, in spite of everything. Was she making a terrible mistake? Evie didn't have any connection with her. Mia knew nothing about her either. But how could she go back to Whitecross now? What was there for her now? Too late. She'd crossed the threshold into another life already.

She rummaged in the rucksack for the two postcards she'd bought in the market. One showed the bridge, the other was of the church at the top of the town. She found her pen and started to write.

Sorry, Dad, I'm going away with some friends. We're going to travel for a bit, but not far and don't come after me, please. I promise you I'm safe, and fine, and you don't need to worry. I'll write again soon. Love Mia.

*

She wrote the address, then started the second one.

Dear Becky, I'm going away. I expect you know already. Sorry if Dad's been hassling you for information. I walked out of the hospital. I'm going to have the baby after all. Don't be mad with me. Missing you. I'll phone soon. Mia.

How definite it looked, written down like that. It cleared her head to see her handwriting on the white card. Black on white. The pressure like a hand pushing down on her head began to lift.

She'd go with Evie. She would have somewhere to stay at least, and it would be a long while before they actually got to Bristol. She should just get on with it. Make the best of everything. Be helpful to Evie. Think what to say to Mum. Or maybe Evie would let her stay? Perhaps Shannon would stay with Joe and then there'd be room for Mia on the boat with Evie? She crawled under the blanket on the couch and drifted into sleep for the rest of the afternoon.

CHAPTER SEVENTEEN

Now there was a new rhythm for her days. Mostly it revolved around the stove and the engine: stoking, keeping the fire going, checking, re-filling with diesel. Keeping warm. Making food. The engine throbbed like a beating heart, a constant sound that soon became part of her, so she only noticed when it stopped. Evie seemed brighter now they'd got on to the canal and were moving slowly along. They were making good progress, Evie said. She seemed to have got used to the idea that Shannon wasn't there, and Mia was doing her best to be helpful.

Most days Evie spent drinking, smoking, even while she was steering the boat. Mia began to wonder where she got the money from. It didn't seem to add up. What else might she be selling, as well as the Indian stuff, the hair braids and tattoos? Mia did not want to think about it. And Evie's mood swung dramatically, one day to another. She was worst at night. Mia started to go to bed earlier to avoid the long, dark silences.

Evie was oddly forgetful too. On the third day they were sitting together in a rare moment of warm sunshine on the deck, drinking tea before they started up for the morning. A woman walked past them along the towpath pushing a small child in a buggy and it reminded Mia about Lainey.

'So how did you get to meet Lainey?'

'Who?'

'You know, the little girl in Ashton.'

'What little girl?'

'You know, who brought me the first time to your boat.'

Evie just shook her head. 'I don't remember. I first saw you around town in that awful shopping precinct where Shannon and I had the stall. You were always hanging about by yourself. We noticed you because you looked too thin, and scared. Like you were in trouble.'

'Was it so obvious?'

'Only to us. Because we've been there. Know what it looks like.'

'What do you mean?'

'Well, Shannon, she was pregnant about your age. She had a baby too, once. That's why she's hanging around Joe so much. Wanted to stay longer with him.'

'I don't understand.'

'She's desperate. For a baby. She fancies Joe, thinks he might be a good bet. For a baby.' Evie's face clouded over. She stared absently for a few minutes. Then she seemed to come back to Mia from wherever she'd been. 'It's hard for her around you, I think. You didn't even want a baby, but you got pregnant just like that. And she hasn't.'

'What happened to the baby?'

'You don't want to know, Mia.'

'Yes I do.'

'Well, she wouldn't want me to tell you.'

'Can't you tell me about it? Just a bit?'

'Well, you mustn't tell Shannon. It's too awful. No, I can't tell you.'

'Please, Evie.'

'You won't like it.'

'Please.'

'I warned you, remember. It's not very nice.' Evie's face darkened. Mia could feel her own heart thumping, not sure what she was about to hear.

'She was only about eleven months. Eden, we called her. She was just beginning to walk, you know, pulling herself up on things and taking a few steps, and you have to watch them all the time then, but

Shannon was in a bit of a state. I didn't really realize, otherwise I could have helped more.'

Evie's eyes filled with tears.

'She wasn't coping, I suppose. Drinking too much, and getting stoned most of the time, and not eating properly. The baby – Eden – well, we don't really know what happened, but she must have got out on the deck when Shannon was out of her head down in the cabin.'

'Oh no – no –'

'I told you you didn't want to know.'

Mia waited, horrified, for what she now knew was coming.

'She must have fallen in. It's easy enough, there's no edge or anything up here. It was the river, not the canal. Not your river, at Ashton. Further north. It was in the papers and everything. About three, four years ago. They didn't find the baby's body for ages. It got washed up at some weir, eventually. It was terrible. So now you know.'

Mia watched the innocent green water of the canal as the boat bobbed on its mooring. It didn't bear thinking about. A small child, slipping over the edge. No one hears the splash. Circles of ripples; a spiral of bubbles. Silence.

Poor, poor Shannon. How did you carry on after something like that?

Evie and Mia watched two damsel flies hovering along the line of reeds. A moorhen scuttled out from under the bank.

'So, what's going on with Shannon and Joe?'

'He's not really interested. Doesn't want to be tied down with a child. Who does?'

Mia frowned.

'Sorry, but you'll find out. You don't think so now. But you will.' Evie started to untie the mooring rope. Mia took the empty mugs back down into the darkness of the cabin.

No I won't. It'll be different with me and my baby.

Mia curled herself up tighter on the bed. She rubbed a space in the condensation on the window and looked outside on to the canal. The water was smooth, not like the fast flowing river they'd left behind.

The small child toddles along the uneven deck. Ducks squabble among the reeds. A swan, perhaps, hisses at the hand stretched out towards it. Then the splash, the flailing arms. Bubbles.

Up till now Mia had felt quite settled, almost comfortable with Evie, in spite of her moods. Today though it felt different. There was a new note in Evie's voice. An edginess in the way she moved. Mia wondered again what had happened to her. What sort of 'trouble' she'd been in. Was her story as terrible as Shannon's?

The more she thought about it, the less it seemed to make sense. Shannon hadn't seemed like someone who'd lost a baby like that. The way she'd talked to Mia. You could tell she liked the idea of Mia's baby, was a bit jealous even, but not like someone who'd had a baby and it had died. If anything, it was Evie who seemed to be the troubled one. The moody one. *What if*, Mia started to wonder, *what if it was Evie's own story she'd just told, and not Shannon's at all?* She shivered.

She ought to go up and help Evie on deck, but instead she got out the two new postcards she'd bought at the post office in the last town they'd travelled through.

Dear Dad, just want you to know I'm still OK, but I'm sorry for all the trouble and I miss you. I don't have any money left so could you put some in my account and I promise I will pay you back when I can get a job or something. Love Mia.

She turned the second one over. She was about to write *Dear Becky*, but on impulse she wrote *Will* instead.

*

Dear Will, how's things? Miss you lots. Think of me next time you go along the beach. Pick up a pebble and wish me luck. Mia.

Writing their names made them feel closer. She put the cards in her pocket ready to post next time they stopped. She liked the feel of the card against her leg, a sort of connection with Will and Dad, reminding her they were there. Even as she travelled further away.

Instead of backs of offices and houses and narrow gardens stretching down to the scruffy towpath, they'd now reached open countryside. The canal kept parallel with a road for a while longer; heavy lorries whined up the hill and there was a background hum of traffic, but soon the canal wound in a broad curve along the valley bottom away from the main road and the only sounds were the engine throb and the gently swooshing of water against the bows. Mia went out on to the front deck. It was cold this morning, although the sun was shining through a thin veil of cloud. She could see her breath. White puffs of smoke.

Dragon's breath, they used to call it on frosty mornings when they walked down the lane to the primary school at Whitecross. Dad walked them down there, Mia, Laura and Kate, and usually he carried Mia's bag because she was the littlest and got tired. He'd be there again in the afternoon, waiting in the playground in the sea of mums. He was quite a novelty: not many other fathers did the daily pick up. The women teased and joked with him and it made Mia cross even though she didn't know why back then. She didn't know the word *flirting*, which Kate used accusingly.

Back then, the three of them were still waiting for Mum to return. They expected her any day. They hadn't understood that she was never coming back. When Mia ran out of her classroom at the end of the day, she'd throw her book bag into Dad's stomach, and he'd whisk her up in his arms and hold her close. He didn't say how much he was missing Mum. None of them did. When they walked back up the lane Dad held her small hand in his large one. '*Car coming!*' he'd yell, and they would squeeze into the hedgerow out of the way. She could feel his body trembling as he pressed her back from the edge. Danger, safety. Always the two together, one edged around with the other.

Mia wrapped her fleece round her tighter. She hadn't thought about all those things Dad had done for her in a long while.

Ahead of the barge, mist rose like steam above the

water. A moorhen peeped and scurried into the reed bank. On both sides of the canal the view opened up on to fields and distant hills. Hardly a house in sight now, just the odd cluster of farm buildings and every so often a stone bridge over the canal where a lane crossed over.

Mia watched the way sun reflected off the water on to the stone sides of the bridge in ripples of light. She was beginning to notice things she would never have bothered with before. Moving so slowly, the little things that changed seemed more important. Underneath, though, the bubble of worry was growing. How much longer could she really keep going like this, on Evie's boat, with no money and no idea how to get any? She still hadn't phoned Mum to say she was coming. In her own mind, she couldn't see further than the long line of canals and rivers crisscrossing the map. She couldn't imagine ever reaching anywhere.

'Do you want to steer for a bit?' Evie called from the back of the boat. Mia edged her way along the side, balancing herself. She'd got used to the feeling now, was less scared that she'd tip backwards into the water. She knew it wasn't very deep, even if she did; nothing like the river that would whirl you along and under as if you were a dead branch or a bundle of rags.

Or a drowning baby.

Evie sat in the open doorway while Mia took the tiller.

It was an easy straight stretch of water. She plucked up courage to talk again.

'Evie? Would you tell me? What happened to you? You said you'd both been in trouble. You and Shannon.'

Evie sighed. 'Very boring. You don't want to know.'

'Yes I do. Please.'

'Not now. Not right after telling you about Shannon. Another day maybe. See how I feel.'

CHAPTER EIGHTEEN

October 25th

'The baby's head is becoming more rounded and it has eyelids. Its muscles are developing and it is moving about inside the uterus much more. It is now about 6.5 cm long, but still weighs only 18 g.'

Another morning, clear and sunny. The air was chilled though. Mia had to borrow an extra jumper from Evie's bag of charity-shop clothes. After breakfast, they settled themselves on the deck and Mia knew Evie was getting herself ready to talk.

'Ready then? My story this morning.'

Mia nodded. She was scared she might say the wrong thing and put her off, so she kept quiet. Evie talked in a flat, low voice, without expression. She didn't look at Mia the whole time.

'Well, it starts with the usual things. Loathing school. Couldn't see the point. Teachers on another planet. So I missed lessons, bunked off, hung around the town. Like you, only this wasn't Ashton.'

Evie stopped talking for so long that Mia thought she'd forgotten what she was saying. She didn't like to remind her. She watched Evie disappear back down into the cabin for a while; heard the hiss of a can being opened and the scrape of a match. She came back on to the deck and settled herself again.

'Still listening?' Evie's voice was harsh. Mia nodded.

'So it got worse. I couldn't do any of the work any more and the teachers hated me for messing up. I didn't get any of my exams. But I wasn't stupid, don't think that.' Evie's face was dark and her voice thick with hate. 'My dad went mad and beat me up and made my mum cry. They were always arguing, anyway, but it got worse then. My dad said get a job or else. Well, in the end I just left. I stayed on friends' floors to begin with, in squats and stuff, but it's harder than you think, never any money, and people offer you drink and a smoke and it helps to begin with, makes you forget, you stop feeling so much – you don't want to hear this, Mia.'

'Yes I do.'

'Well, maybe I don't want to talk about it any more. That's enough. That's it, anyway. Things got bad. But they're much better now, I mean, look at this beautiful boat –' Evie stretched her arms out. 'What more could you want? Never have to stay put, you just move on. Wonderful views, new people to meet.'

What more could you want? Mia could think of plenty of things. But she wouldn't say, not to Evie. Evie had been generous and kind to Mia. She didn't have much, but she shared it anyway. It didn't seem the right time to ask *how* she'd got the boat. And there were other gaps in Evie's story. The more she thought about it, the more Mia felt convinced that what Evie had said about Shannon's baby was really about her own. Maybe she could ask Shannon when she turned up with Joe. If she did, of course.

Evie was lost in daydreams again. Perhaps Mia had made a mistake asking about the past. '*Everyone has a story,*' Evie had said the first time she met them on the river. But stories come in different versions. And they're not always happy.

'I'm going to have a lie down.' Evie's face was closed over; she'd opened up a bit and now she was firmly locked up again. 'Give us a shout when you see the next village or town or wherever. We need food and diesel probably. And we should wait up for Shannon, I guess. We don't want to get too far ahead. Safer to stick together.'

Mia watched Evie disappear into the dark cabin.

She saw the thin curls of cigarette smoke hanging in the air where she'd been. The boat would stink of it. She hated that. It made her anxious too, thinking of Evie smoking on the bed, dropping ash. After a few drinks, she was less careful.

Evie didn't seem to like the way Shannon hung out with Joe. Perhaps she was jealous? What she said was that it 'wasn't good for Shannon'. She treated Shannon a bit like a mother might. *Some mothers might*, Mia corrected herself. Because mothers weren't all the same, were they?

But what if it was really the other way round? If it was Shannon keeping an eye on Evie? Evie who'd lost the baby?

Evie's bad mood persisted. She'd finished the cans of cider and beer and smoked her way through her cigarettes, and they still hadn't got to any town or even a pub. Mia carried on steering the boat, even though her arms ached and she longed to lie down.

Evie sat in the open doorway and picked at Mia, finding fault with everything.

'Why haven't you talked to your mum then? . . . What are you going to do when you get there?'

Mia was silent, biting back tears.

'What about your school work then?' Evie started up again.

'I dunno. I'm not thinking about that now.'

'No, but you should. You don't want to end up like me, do you?'

'Why not? You said yourself you've got everything you want – your boat, friends.'

'That's not what I said. I said it was better than it was. In any case, we wouldn't have the boat if it weren't for Shannon's brother. He bought it. He's loaded. He's an accountant or something. Not that she ever sees him. You should get your exams. Once we get you to Bristol. Get a job, money. Look after your kid. Or will your dad keep on bailing you out?'

Mia flushed and then shrugged. 'I want to be able to manage myself.'

'Well, you won't get a decent job without your exams, will you?'

'I can go to college later, can't I? I don't want to think about it now. I thought you were on my side!' Mia turned away angrily.

'Watch the boat! Idiot!' Evie jumped up to grab the tiller as the boat juddered towards the bank. Mia cowered, crouched on the tiny deck space. For a moment she hated Evie, and the boat.

'Stop feeling sorry for yourself. You have to keep your mind on the boat if you're steering. Grow up, Mia. Start taking responsibility for something.'

'Shut up! You've no right.'

'No? Why not? You're on my boat, eating my food, wearing my clothes. I'm doing you one huge favour, remember?'

'I didn't ask you to, you suggested it!' Mia's eyes brimmed with hot tears. She didn't have to put up with this! But the boat was tiny – and surrounded by water – and there was nowhere else to be, nothing but fields and trees and hills as far as the eye could see. Nowhere to run. She was trapped. Her head ached and her throat stung with tears she wouldn't let out.

Evie seemed to pull herself together. She took back the helm of the boat and steered competently towards the bridge ahead, slowed the engine, then increased speed slightly once they were through.

Mia pushed past her into the cabin and lay on the unmade bed. It stank of stale cigarettes, beer, sweat. She felt sick. Disgusted. She cried into the pillow until her eyes were sore and red. The boat chugged on, slowly, steadily taking her further away from everything she knew. *Too far now. No going back.*

Evie acted as if nothing had happened. Much later, she called down to Mia to make tea. Mia surprised herself by getting on with it. Doing as she was told. There wasn't any other option really.

When she carried the mug of tea out to Evie, Evie smiled and said softly, 'I *am* on your side, Mia. That's the whole point. I want to help you. You and your baby.'

Thinking about it afterwards, there was something, Mia thought, not quite right. Something slightly menacing in the softly spoken words. *I want to help you. You and your baby.* It niggled at her.

Mia pulled the covers over the couch where she'd been dozing and looked through her small rucksack of things. She put the notebook down on the couch, then fished out her purse. Only about one pound fifty left; it was surprising how much food cost, and fuel. And the cans of beer, for Evie, and cigarettes. Mia couldn't really say no when she asked. Evie was sharing her home, giving up her time, making the whole journey for Mia. She fingered the small gold key in her purse. Her front door key, although she wouldn't be needing it now, would she? *I've left for good. I didn't really mean to, but somehow it just happened.* Dad would say that's how she did everything. *Drifting. You never think about the consequences, do you?*

There was no key for the *Dragonfly*.

'We don't lock the boat,' Evie had said. 'There's nothing to steal anyway. It's much better not to lock doors. Then there's nothing to batter down.'

'But aren't you scared? On your own at night?' Mia asked.

'Of what? There's nothing can happen that hasn't already.'

Mia went cold right through when Evie said that. Her own worst imaginings seemed bad enough, but she sensed there were more things Evie wouldn't tell her, things she couldn't even imagine. It made her frightened. The darkness in Evie, alongside the kindness. What happened if the balance tipped?

Why was she helping Mia? What was it she really wanted from her? A sudden dart of fear shot in and lodged itself deep under her ribs. It wouldn't go.

Now the boat bobbed against the bank while Evie tied the ropes on to the stake in the grass bank. She had spotted a stack of logs in the woodland running alongside the canal.

'Perfect. Dry firewood. For free.'

'But they look like they belong to someone. They're all stacked up properly under a shelter, Evie.'

'Well, there's plenty to go round. No one here now. We'll take what we need for the stove. They won't miss them. Anyway, you can't own trees and woods. Common ground, common property.'

Mia thought of herself at eleven, nicking sweets at the corner shop. Fourteen, stashing cans of lager under her school jumper in the off-licence while the others distracted the girl at the counter. It wasn't her fault she never had any money. *It was just for fun. Just a dare. Not really stealing, was it? So what was different about this?*

'Come on, Mia. If we stock up on wood we won't have to spend so much on coal.'

Mia helped Evie carry armloads of logs on to the path. They were too big for the stove, and had to be chopped and split with the axe into smaller pieces. Mia and Evie took turns. The axe handle made her hands sting and blister. Her shoulders ached. It grew colder as the afternoon wore on, and Mia got slower and weaker. In the end, Evie took over all the chopping and Mia just stood around, feeling useless again. She tried to think of how else she could help.

'I can – well, probably – get some more money out in a day or so.' Mia bit her lip anxiously. 'Once Dad's got my card. I asked him, you know, to put some in my account. The child-benefit money, that's for me, so it's my money really.'

Evie laughed, scornful. 'Thought you wanted to manage on your own? Anyway, if you keep writing to him he'll work out where you are, won't he? He'll see the postmarks all joined together, a string of places along the canal as clear as a map, stupid. He'll be coming after you, take you back home. Or is that what you want?' She glared at Mia. 'Don't you want to make a go of this? Be free for once and do what *you* want?'

That's what *she* had done. But what if it wasn't the right thing for Mia? It had been her dad who'd looked after her all those years, not her mum. Already she saw him a bit differently, just twelve days away from him. And the horrible letter from Mum still lay crumpled in her bag. She still hadn't told Evie what it said.

'It's cold enough for frost,' Evie announced.

They made a fire on the bank, heaping up logs to make a huge blaze of flames. Their pale faces glowed in the orange light. Witch faces, Mia thought. Hollow eyes, dark spaces. The magic of the fire was irresistible; they danced round it, whooping into the darkness and silence that lay just outside the circle of light. Then, as it died down, they arranged logs around it to sit on and warmed themselves, front first, turning round every so often to warm their backs. Mia stopped worrying whether anyone would see the fire and come and find them. There was no one for miles. The sky was black, deep velvet pinned with stars. Frost was already beginning to form, a silver edging to dead leaves, grasses, puddles along the towpath. The boat deck too, had a white shadow of ice.

'In winter, when it's really cold for days on end,

the canal freezes over. You can get stuck for days.'
Evie stirred the white ashes in the fire. 'We'll stoke up
the stove in the cabin when this has died down and
get it properly warm for the night. We might as well
moor here all night. Shannon and Joe will probably
be here by morning.'

'They won't be travelling in the dark surely?'

'No. But we've been going really slowly, and they'll
probably get up earlier than us tomorrow and try and
catch up.'

'What if she's not coming after all?'

Evie snapped at Mia. 'Course she is. Where else is
she going to go? Joe won't want her. Not for long.'

Mia didn't risk an answer. She was exhausted after
the afternoon on the canal bank. No more arguments,
she thought. Please. She'd go to bed early. There was
nothing to do anyway, except talk to Evie or read,
and she didn't feel like doing either. She dozed in
the light from the stove for a while. Every so often
Evie opened the glass front and shoved in more logs.
The cabin was hot at last; the sweet smell of wood
smoke mixed with the oils Evie burned over a small
candle flame. Mia turned over on her side and shut
her eyes. She could hear the spit and crackle of logs
shifting, and the thin rasp of pages being turned as
Evie read her book, and then she slept.

*

Mia woke, sweating and struggling. She tugged at the blankets, which had somehow wound round her body as she tossed and turned in sleep, binding her too tight. The heat was unbearable. She could feel beads of sweat around her hairline and neck. She was still half in her dream – a horrible, torturing nightmare, where Evie, bigger and more frightening than in real life, held Mia prisoner on the boat so that she could steal her baby and give it to Shannon. In the dream she was clutching at the baby all bundled up in blankets and they were pulling it away from her, tugging at the blankets so hard they pulled them right out of her arms and the bundle unrolled and there was suddenly nothing, no baby there – and then the three of them were leaning over the edge of the boat, their hands scrabbling in the green water and the tangled weeds, searching for a baby turned fish.

Mia untangled herself and sat up. She placed one hand on her chest, felt the birdwing flapping frantically there. Too real. In the sweaty darkness it seemed all too possible that Evie and Shannon had planned this all along, and she had been too stupid, too afraid to see what was happening.

Across the cabin, Evie slept and snored, oblivious. She looked innocent enough, but what could you ever tell by looking?

Mia must have gone back to sleep because the next

time she woke to find herself coughing. She was still way too hot, even though she'd pushed the covers off her body. This time though there was something seriously wrong; she could sense it. Mia was wide awake now, not dozy like she'd been before. The dark was different, not black but fogged and blurred and the smell she knew at once was of smoke – not the sweet wood-smoke smell, but the sour, choking poison of smouldering cloth, chair-stuffing, foam rubber.

'Evie? Evie! Something's burning. Quick! Wake up!'

CHAPTER NINETEEN

October 26th

*W*hy wouldn't Evie wake up? Mia shook the sleeping body and at last she stirred, but she seemed confused, her speech slurred. How much had she had to drink after Mia went to sleep? What else had she taken? Tablets or something? Evie tried to turn back on her side to sleep again. Mia kept on shaking her.

'Evie, wake up! Something's burning. The couch.' Mia coughed and spluttered. They needed air – *quick* – she could hardly breathe. She struggled in the darkness towards the doors at the back of the cabin and fumbled for the catch. As she pushed the door open she realized her mistake. The rush of freezing air into the cabin fed the smouldering fire and a line of small flames licked quickly along the edge of the couch where Evie was still slumped. *Water – get the bucket and fill it from the canal.* There was no shortage of water at least, but first she must drag Evie off the burning couch and out into the air.

Evie was a dead weight. She wouldn't wake up properly.

'Please, Evie! You have to help. I can't manage it.' Mia's voice shook with fear.

But Evie seemed not to recognize her, seemed to think that Mia was trying to hurt her. She flailed out with her arms and tried to burrow back under the blankets.

The cabin was full of smoke; clouds of it caught in the moonlight that flooded in through the open doors. The air fanned the flames and they licked across the fabric to where Evie lay.

She had to get Evie out of there quickly. Mia tugged and pulled and gradually, bit by bit, dragged the woman closer to the open door and fresher air. Then she went back to beat out the flames. She tried to smother them with the blanket from her bed, but the smoke was so foul she couldn't stay inside the cabin long enough and she was forced to crawl back to the deck for air. She found the bucket at last, and scooped it into the canal, carried it half full, in shaking arms, and threw it over the couch. Over and over she repeated the action, her arms numb and her throat raw from smoke. But at last the flames went out, and then she tugged the whole foam mattress, charred and smoking and sodden, out through the doorway on to the deck.

Evie watched her, coughing, her eyes hollow and empty.

Mia wept silently with exhaustion and misery. She'd had to do it all, by herself. Evie was somewhere far off, locked in some private misery, incapable of action. They could have burned to death in their beds and no one would have seen the glowing boat on the still water, no one would have called for help. She shook and shivered and coughed, and finally slumped down next to Evie on the freezing deck and put her arm round Evie's shoulders.

'You're OK. You'll be fine. It's all OK now. Come on, Evie. We'll go back in and make you a bed and you can sleep it off.' She felt Evie's body trembling through the layers of jumpers. She looked like a small child, Mia thought. Like Lainey or someone. A little girl wearing too big clothes. Pretending to be grown up.

The cabin stank of foul smoke, even with all the doors open, and now it felt freezing, even under layers of covers and jumpers. Mia wanted to sleep and sleep, but every time she closed her eyes she thought she smelled burning again, or heard the faint trickle of a flame stirring somewhere. Her thoughts went round, over and over the same. She could have died. If she hadn't been there, Evie would have suffocated from smoke, sunk too deep in her drugged sleep. She had to get out of here. Evie was too deep in something she didn't really understand, didn't want to know. It wasn't good for Mia, it wasn't safe; and what damage was it doing to her baby? Little bean. She hadn't thought about little bean all through the fire. She ached all over, down to the pit of her belly.

Finally, as it began to get light, she dozed and slept at last.

Mia woke up desperate for the loo. She groped her way to the tiny compartment where they kept the Elsan. She wrinkled up her nose at the chemical smell. Then, horrified, she stared at the paper in her hand, at the small red smear. Even in the grey half-light she knew what it was. She was bleeding.

Mia lay back down, wrapped herself in the blanket and cried. Back in September, she had watched and waited for blood that never came. Each day she'd counted and watched and waited. Now it was beginning, and the sight of it filled her with fear and horror and loathing. So was this it? Somehow she had damaged her body, all that carrying and heaving, first Evie and then the unbearable weight of the buckets of water, and the cold, and the fear . . . and had she made the baby die?

She was freezing. The stove had gone out. Why wasn't Evie up and doing things? Mia hated her, the dark shape that was her humped-up body under the covers, snuffling and whimpering in her sleep. No use to anyone. Mia scrabbled around for her bag and found the old pregnancy book. She turned the pages, looking for what to do. There was a whole chapter on losing a baby. She read what it said about a threatened miscarriage. '*Stop everything and go to bed.*' Then she read what it said about '*inevitable abortion . . . a miscarriage that occurs because the baby is no longer alive. Whatever you do and however much you rest, the bleeding is bound to continue.*' The only way to tell was to see if there was a foetal heartbeat – by having an ultrasound scan, in hospital. Or you could just wait and see.

Mia lay on her back, her hands curved round her belly. It had stopped aching. Was that a good sign or a bad one? She tried not to think about the trickle of blood. Was there more? She couldn't be sure. She turned all her attention inside herself, willing little bean to be all right. *Please, please, please. I'll do anything. I'll go back home – anything.*

Gradually she became aware of sounds outside the boat. Morning on the canal. Coots and moorhens, songbirds in the woodland. A pigeon, cooing. Then a new sound. Chug, chugging of a distant engine.

Coming closer? A boat? A little bubble of hope rose to the surface. But what if they went straight past, without stopping? She staggered out to the deck to flag them down.

Joe's boat. Mia recognized the bright blue paintwork, the sacks of coal on the roof, and there – Shannon at the tiller, guiding the boat alongside and waving with one hand.

Her face changed as she caught sight of the charred mattress and the smoke-stained doors and windows of *Dragonfly,* and Mia's ashen face.

'*What the –?*'

'There was a fire.'

'Are you both OK? Where's Evie?'

'Inside. She's sleeping. She won't wake up properly. I don't know if she's OK or not – and –'

'Joe?' Shannon yelled down to the cabin. 'Quick! There's been a fire. Take this.' Shannon threw her the rope, jumped over on to *Dragonfly,* and went into the cabin. Mia secured the rope and followed.

Shannon got the stove going while Mia told her what had happened.

'You shouldn't take any risks,' she told Mia, making her lie down again. 'You ought to go to a hospital and get checked out.'

Mia nodded.

'Evie's in a state. She gets like this. I shouldn't have stayed with Joe. I knew she wasn't happy.' She stroked the hair back from Evie's forehead. 'I'll sort her out a bit. Then we can take you to the next town. How far is it?'

Mia shook her head. 'I dunno. We had a map somewhere.' She rooted about half-heartedly in the pile of books and papers she'd shoved out of the way in a bag in the kitchen area. Shannon tutted impatiently. Finally Mia found it, damp and scrunched up, and they spread it out on the floor.

'I think we're about here.' Shannon pointed to a straight stretch of canal. She showed Mia the wood, and the little squares that meant farm buildings.

'So it's about twelve miles to a big enough town.' She looked at Mia. 'Or you could get to the next pub and phone someone. A taxi? To the hospital? Your mum?'

Mia shook her head.

'Don't be stupid. Don't you want this baby?' She glowered at Mia.

Mia's eyes were full of tears. The lump of fear under her ribs expanded a little; her heart beat a little faster.

'Yes. I do.' Her voice came out too quiet. She hesitated. 'What's wrong with Evie?'

'Overdose, probably. Alcohol and tablets. Stupid.

She's done it before. You're best out of here, Mia. You don't want to get mixed up in Evie's mess.'

'What happened to her? Was there a baby?'

'What did she tell you? About the baby? I knew I should have stayed with her.'

'She said it was you. You that had the baby – who died. Drowned. But it wasn't, was it?'

'She said *what*?'

'I sort of guessed it wasn't. That it must have been her. It made it easier for her to tell me, I suppose, pretending it had happened to you.'

'Oh, Mia! What a mess!'

'But she said things were better now, and it all seemed so lovely, the boat, and everything, till then.'

'Well. Now you know. Things happen to people. You don't leave them behind that easy.' Shannon turned her back on Mia and went on stroking Evie's face. 'I think she'll be OK. When she wakes up properly. How did the fire start?'

'I'm not sure. The candles, maybe? Or she was smoking?'

Shannon nodded. 'I've told her before. But when she gets down she forgets stuff. Lucky you woke up.'

'Yes.'

Mia watched Shannon stroking Evie's cheek, smoothing back her hair. Like a mother might. The two women were close in a way Mia could hardly understand. It would be like her and Becky perhaps, if they'd been through something terrible together. A giving and taking of comfort, but shared, not just one way. Taking turns to be the strong one. Sometimes the mother, sometimes the child. Mia wasn't close to her sisters or her mum. But maybe that didn't matter so much. It didn't mean she'd never be close to anyone.

'Perhaps we should get a doctor?' Mia suggested. Shannon shook her head.

'No way. Once you get caught up with that lot, they start taking over. Saying you're not fit, need medication. It's a slippery slope. Evie's been there. She was in hospital before. After the baby. You know, *the mental health system*.' She said the words as if they were poisonous. 'She's much better off with me looking after her for a bit. I wonder what got to her. Set this off again?'

Mia immediately felt guilty. She said nothing.

'We'll move her on to Joe's boat when she wakes up. It's disgusting in here now, what with all the smoke and damp. You must have shifted bucket-loads of water. No wonder you're bleeding. Is it stopping?'

'I'm not sure. I think so.'

'Well, stay lying down a bit longer. Then we'll sort you out.'

CHAPTER TWENTY

October 27th

You're going to be all right. Hang on in there, little bean.

Mia chanted the words like a mantra. *It's a good sign that the sun's shining. If that bird stays on the fencepost until I reach the next tree it means everything's going to be fine.* She willed the little bird to stay. It flew off just as she reached the tree. *What does that mean?*

It felt good to be walking along the sunny towpath instead of being crouched up on the boat. The bleeding seemed to have stopped; she'd rested all the day before, and Joe and Shannon had looked after her. She'd felt better as soon as she'd woken up this morning.

Shannon had said to go gently, not too fast, but Mia couldn't stop herself hurrying along the path. She could see the pub buildings across the field now;

soon she'd be making the phone call and then maybe she could stop worrying for a while.

She'd only packed a few things in the rucksack: the book, and a change of clothes, and her notebook. She'd let Evie think she'd be coming back. But maybe Shannon had guessed. She'd encouraged her to go, after all, first thing that morning.

'Goodbye,' she said as Mia left the boats. 'Good luck.'

Mia had been surprised; she'd had that horrible dream again in the night, where the two boat women snatched her baby from her and then dropped it, so that it slipped over the edge. She'd half expected Shannon to stop her getting off the boat in the morning, instead of encouraging her. Keeping her prisoner. Now, in the bright morning light, it all just seemed like some silly night-time fantasy.

She only had one twenty-pence piece. And a ten-pound note that Joe had given her. That meant just one phone call. It was one of the old-fashioned red boxes outside the pub. Mia went inside. She knew the number off by heart. She hesitated, staring at the laminated display of local numbers next to the national dialling codes. She took a deep breath. *I want to manage on my own*: her words to Evie. *Or will your dad keep on bailing you out?*

It must still be morning. The pub wasn't open. Dad would be at work. So would Mum.

She dialled the number for a taxi, and sat down on the stone bench to wait.

The driver made her pay up front. Didn't trust her. She saw herself through his eyes: white-faced, dark hollow eyes, unwashed spiky hair, muddy trousers, stinking of smoke. Hands blackened from soot. He didn't speak the entire journey, deposited her at the hospital gate and drove off with a melodramatic squeal of brakes, as if he couldn't get rid of her fast enough, muttering obscenities under his breath. She'd better get used to it, Mia thought. The hospital staff might treat her the same way. She pushed her way through heavy swing doors and into the Accident and Emergency department.

A blonde-haired woman at reception stared at her. Mia walked up to the desk, wishing she was not blushing as the woman took in her muddy clothes and unwashed hair.

'Name?'

'Mia.'

'Spelt?'

'M – I – A.'

'Second name? Address?'

'Kitson. No address. Well, a boat. It moves about.'

'You have to have an address.' The woman was determined not to smile. She seemed to think Mia was being deliberately difficult.

Mia thought fast. 'My mum's then.' She rummaged through her bag, searching out the letter with the address in Bristol.

The woman frowned as she wrote it down. 'And you're here for what?' She stared at the form she was filling in, refusing eye contact.

'Threatened miscarriage.'

The telephone rang. The woman waved towards the rows of chairs. 'There'll be a long wait. You're not exactly an emergency.'

Mia could guess what she really thought. It would be better if Mia lost the baby. Some stupid teenage dropout who should have been in school. A waste of space. Waste of NHS money.

She sat down next to the window and looked around. A few old dossers sleeping in chairs. A woman with three kids, one of them crying on her lap. A man holding his finger in a wodge of tissues. Sunlight streamed through the tall window and lit up the fur of dust on the sill and the floor. You'd expect a hospital to be clean, but this one wasn't. Mia watched the blue sky through the windows, and the way the squares of sunlight moved across the floor. People came and went; phones rang. An ambulance arrived, sirens squealing, and for a moment the whole hospital seemed to come alive with people in white coats running with clipboards and machines.

Finally it was her turn. A male nurse took her to a small room and told her to take off her shoes and lie on the high couch. He smiled at the mud on her trainers. 'What've you been up to then?'

Mia tried to smile back. 'I'm living on a boat.'

He listened while she told him about the fire. 'The doctor'll be here in a minute. She'll sort you out. Don't worry.' His voice was kind.

Mia lay on the couch. The nurse went out into the corridor. She heard feet tap tapping along the corridor, and then low voices. She supposed he was telling the doctor about her. The cubicle door opened and the nurse came back in with a young woman, short dark hair.

She held her hand out and smiled at Mia. 'I'm Dr Sabir.'

She felt Mia's tummy and asked questions. Mia lied when she asked her age. Said she was sixteen. You could leave home at sixteen. Have sex. Get married even, if you were that stupid.

'How many weeks? Twelve or thirteen? It's quite normal to have little bleeds like this in pregnancy. Sometimes around the time you would have been having a period. But we'll get the portable scanner in here to check the baby out and reassure you. And you've been through quite a hard time, Mia, so I think we should check you out too.' It was a relief to be spoken to as if she was an intelligent human being after all.

They left her for a while, to drink a whole jug of water. A full bladder made it possible for the ultrasound to create images of the baby in her womb.

Back on the couch, Mia lay anxiously while the doctor rubbed a jelly-like substance over her tummy. 'Sorry it's a bit cold. They normally warm it up if you have a scan in Antenatal. OK, Mia? Try to relax.'

She felt the firm circular movements as the doctor moved the transducer over her belly, pressing down too hard over her bladder so she squeaked.

'Sorry.'

Mia watched the doctor's face, searching for signs. She frowned, and Mia's mouth tightened. She held her breath. Her heart pounded. The doctor seemed to go over and over the same place, pushing at her abdomen until it felt almost sore. Mia's fists clenched at her side, and she felt the nurse reach out and uncurl one hand, holding it in his. What could they see? Why didn't they say something? For a wild moment Mia wondered if there was perhaps nothing at all. An empty womb. Or a shrivelled-up foetus, died long ago, a hard walnut of blackened tissue.

'OK,' the doctor said. 'Everything's fine. Want to see?'

The doctor swivelled round the small screen so Mia could see it if she strained to one side. A fuzzy black and white scrabble of lines on a screen. The doctor showed her the head. She smiled. 'And that's the heart. Beating fine. And something else moving. An arm, I think. Hard to see on this small machine. You'd get a better picture down on the full-sized machines in Antenatal.'

But it was enough for Mia. Tears trickled down her cheeks and pooled in her ears. She tightened her grip on the nurse's hand. There was little bean. That blur on the screen was her baby. Alive. She'd seen her baby. Everything was all right.

They wouldn't let her go home. They wanted to book her into the ward, let her have a shower, get cleaned up, and have a bit of a rest, they said, and they could do a few checks. Blood tests. Make sure she wasn't anaemic. The antenatal ward was full so she would have to go up to Gynaecology. And she'd have to wait a while for a bed there. They asked her again how old she was.

Mia sat on the toilet, trying to think. Shannon's words ran through her head like a stuck CD. '*Once they've got you in the system . . .*'

What could they do? They would phone her mum, for sure. She'd given her address at reception. So stupid. She'd have to do a runner again. Now she knew the baby was OK. And that would be the second escape from a hospital. She'd be getting into deeper trouble. Where could she go? Back to the boat? Evie's semi-unconscious face swam before her. Shannon frowning. *Better off out of here.* Had it been a warning? That dream she'd had: Evie's plan to get a baby for Shannon. Her baby.

She walked slowly towards the exit. *Think of little bean.* The voices chattered in her head, confusing her. She hesitated, turned, saw the male nurse watching her from the end of the corridor. She looked right at him and he looked directly at her. He shook his head slightly, sadly. But what did he know? He'd soon forget her. She was one of thousands. He'd shrug, move on to the next case. They couldn't make her stay in hospital. She was sixteen, wasn't she? – as far as they were concerned anyway. Old enough to make her own choices.

Mia turned away and kept on walking. She already knew what she wanted to do.

CHAPTER TWENTY-ONE

A gang of boys skateboarded past Mia as she stood on the pavement in the crowded bus station, wondering which way to go. One young boy deliberately shoved into Mia as he went by and knocked her bag off her shoulder. Her purse spilled out of the half-zipped top and coins rolled into the gutter.

'Slag!'

The other boys laughed as Mia huddled over, gathering up the scattered coins.

'Are you all right, dear?' An elderly woman in a grey coat tutted and patted Mia's arm kindly.

'I'm OK, thanks.'

Only a few months ago and she would have shouted back at boys like that. Stupid prats. They couldn't be more than twelve or thirteen. She would have been rude to the old lady too. For speaking to her. For interfering. For noticing.

Now, she was just grateful for the tiny bit of kindness in this desolate place. 'Do you know where I can find out –' Mia started asking the woman, but she'd already walked on out of earshot.

Mia made her way towards the concrete buildings in the centre of the bus-station concourse. From a seedy cafe wafted the smell of hot fat, chips, coffee. Eventually she found a departures board nailed to a wall next to the toilets. Lists of buses going to places she'd never heard of. Finally she managed to work out where to go. Two changes, a long wait in the middle. But she should get there before dark.

She was dying for a pee. Just enough time.

The floor was wet and stank of disinfectant. Only a couple of the toilets were working. Neither had seats or paper. A used syringe and a blood-stained roll of tissue poked out of the bin.

Mia stared at her own face in the chipped mirror above the handbasin as she rinsed her hands under the cold tap. She hardly recognized it: the dark shadows, uncombed hair.

Over the shoulder of her reflection a second pale face peered into the mirror.

'Spare any change? So I can get into the night shelter? I need a couple of quid.' The voice was slurred.

Mia dropped her gaze, embarrassed. 'I'm sorry.

I've only just got enough to get home myself.'

Her voice sounded too posh. She wanted the girl to know *it's true, I really haven't*. The girl seemed to crumple down on to the wet floor and started to rock back and forth, mumbling under her breath. Her eyes were wild, crazy. But what could Mia do? She edged out of the loos again.

As she came back out she noticed the ticket inspector near the departures board. Perhaps he could help the girl? The man was trying without success to calm down an angry woman who'd waited nearly an hour for a bus. He waved his hands in despair. 'What can I do? So many drivers off sick.'

'Excuse me,' Mia interrupted, 'but there's a young girl in the loos, collapsed on the floor. I think she needs help.'

He looked at her uncomprehendingly. She repeated her words. He looked more closely at her then, as if she were the one who needed help. But not with pity or compassion. A sort of contempt crawled over his mouth.

'What's new? She's always in there. What do you expect me to do?' He shrugged. 'I've got a job to do and it's not cleaning filth out of toilets.' He turned his back on her and she shrank back, shocked at his outburst.

Mia felt utterly exhausted. It was too much, all

this on top of the horror of the fire and then the hospital. All she wanted was to be somewhere safe, and kind, where she could sleep without looking over her shoulder. She'd uncovered too much – this dark underbelly of life; kids without hope, or dignity, or anything; adults grey with disappointment, numbed out and without heart. Whitecross might be boring, and school a dreary, soul-destroying waste of time, but this – this half life, underground life, was much, much worse. She suddenly longed to be back home. She'd had enough of the greyness, the cold and dirt, the hopelessness, the loneliness of it all. The thought of hot water, clean clothes, a kitchen with food in the cupboard – Dad.

It wasn't running back, was it? Whatever Evie and Shannon had said. Not a giving up of anything? Mia half remembered something Mum had written in that letter. Something about spreading wings, flying free. There was nothing free about this life on the streets, on the move. Not really. And she had to think of a baby now, not just herself. Little bean needed somewhere safe and warm and loving. Not this sort of no-man's land she'd wandered into. You could get lost in this and never find a way out.

Mia put her hand into her fleece pocket and her fingers closed around a small pebble. Will had picked it up on the beach at Whitecross. '*Look . . . Mottled blue, just like a blackbird's egg.*' His gift to her. She cradled the pebble in her palm and felt the smooth surface begin to warm.

When the bus drew into Bay Fourteen Mia stepped on.

CHAPTER TWENTY-TWO

'*What have you been doing today, Mia?*'

'*We did drawings and Mrs Harrison read us a story.*'

'*What did you draw, love?*'

'*We all did a bird, we had to choose one from the book and we're going to stick them up on the wall.*'

'*And what bird did you choose?*'

'*A house martin.*'

'*Why did you choose that?*'

'*Because I liked the colours. Blue and green. It had to be a bird that goes away and comes back.*'

'*A migrating bird.*'

'*Yes.*'

'*I can show you the house martins that come back to the barn each year. They come back to the same nests where they were born. We can walk up there together one evening.*'

'*Will Mum come too?*'

'*You know she won't, Mia. She's not going to be here like that any more.*'

'*She's not going to come back, is she, Daddy?*'

'*No, sweetheart. Well, she'll visit us sometimes maybe. But not back to stay.*'

'*Why not?*'

'*Oh, Mia, not again. Please.*'

'*How do the house martins know where to come back?*'

'*I don't know, sweetheart. A sort of homing instinct. Back to the same place where they were born.*'

'*But what if they get lost?*'

'*Well, maybe some do. Things happen. But most of them come back.*'

The bus rumbled on. Mia drifted in and out of memories, thoughts, dreams, half asleep, lulled by the movement, the backcloth of voices as people greeted one another getting on and off. The bus travelled through small villages, back lanes, farms. Once she glimpsed the canal – a shining silver strip between willow trees.

The fields had changed into tarmacked streets, new estates, then the edges of a town. A load of school-children got on, filled the seats at the back of the bus around Mia. Fragments of conversation floated in and out of Mia's head. 'Homework ... Mr Briggs ... did you see?'

The bus emptied out again, re-filled. Then they were in another town. Time to change buses. Three quarters of an hour to wait.

More roads, houses, fields, the river: nearly at Ashton, at last. The bridge. Mia peered through the steamed-up window. That was where she'd first seen Lainey. She hoped she was somewhere warmer, safer, than the precarious parapet or the lonely streets this cold night.

She'd missed the last bus to Whitecross: she'd have to get one as far as Stonegate and walk from there. Lights on in the bus. A ribbon of road stretching ahead. Sky getting darker, too early for sunset. Grey clouds like a blanket. A flock of seagulls flying in from the sea, settling on the dark ploughed fields. Raw cold. Wind hissing in the edges of the window flaps. Condensation misting the glass.

'Cold enough for snow,' someone said.

Mia rubbed a hole with her sleeve to see through. A circle of field, hedge, stone wall. As it got darker outside, the people on the bus seemed to pull closer together. There was more chatter, laughter. No one Mia recognized: the Whitecross people would have got the bus that went straight through, all the way.

The thought of the walk ahead made her feel tired, even though she'd slept most of the journey. Dad might be home, she could ring him. But no, she didn't want her homecoming to be like that. She'd imagined it already: walking up the lane, into the garden. The lights would be on, but the curtains still undrawn so she'd see into the kitchen, and Dad at the table, probably, with a mug of tea. And she'd ring the bell, even though she had a key, and he would open the door and hold out his arms.

She tried another version. He stands there at the door, barring her way in. *Too late. You ran off, you make your own way. You're not my daughter any more.*

And another. Through the lit window she sees Miss Blackman holding hands with Dad across the kitchen table. They lean forward, kiss. The window is open. She hears their voices. *So glad it's just us two. It couldn't have worked with Mia around. She needed to go. It was all for the best. Now we have each other –*

'Everybody off! End of the road!' The bus driver enjoyed turning them out on to the darkening street. There weren't many houses in Stonegate; just a cluster of older stone buildings near the pub and the church and a sprawl of newer bungalows along the main road. Everyone getting off the bus was old, Mia noticed. Except her.

'Where are you heading, dear?' A woman in a headscarf turned towards Mia.

'Whitecross.'

'It's a bit of a walk, dear. Nearly two miles.'

'I know. I'm OK.'

'Well, if you're sure. It's getting dark.'

'I'm fine. Really.'

She could feel their eyes following her as she humped her bag on to her shoulder and began to walk along the main road. Imagined the gossip. *What a state to get in . . . Did you see how dirty? . . . Youth . . . drugs . . . not in our day . . . somebody's daughter –*

The pavement went as far as the end bungalow, then petered out. There weren't many cars, but they went too fast, whizzing past and swerving out at the last minute as they caught sight of her in the head-lights. She hadn't realized it would get dark so early. The cold lump of fear in her belly grew bigger, more leaden. Too easy for someone not to see, to hit her, not even stop.

The wind was bitter. She crossed the main road and went down a small lane that seemed to be roughly the right direction, towards where the sea must be. Then she could go along the strip of beach that ran the whole way. She wouldn't have to go into Whitecross at all. It took her towards a farm, and then there was a footpath sign. At last. She could hear the scrape and suck of waves on shingle. The path opened out; there was the beach. It was lighter here, away from any trees; the sea reflected back the strange grey light from the clouds. Icy cold.

Mia headed into the wind and crunched along the pebbles in the direction of home. She could see the lights of Whitecross village ahead, tiny pinpricks a very long way off. She had to keep stopping to shift the weight of her bag, and to wipe her eyes where the wind stung them into tears. She hadn't eaten anything for hours. *Keep going. Head down. No choice now. No giving up.* Her and little bean, going home.

Nearly there. Up the lane. Through the open gate. First few scurries of snow driven on the wind. Mia lifted her head. Flakes, like soft white feathers, drifting down.

The house was in darkness.

CHAPTER TWENTY-THREE

Mia sank down on the front step. She'd never imagined this; an empty house. She unzipped the bag and fumbled for her purse and key with numb hands.

She staggered into the hall and collapsed on the floor. For hours, it seemed, she lay half asleep, half dreaming, half hallucinating. Over and over she dreamed she was being swept downstream, and she had to clutch on to overhanging branches that came away in her hands and were swept on with her, further towards the edge. The edge was what? She was too exhausted to care.

Eventually she woke up enough to think of getting out of her wet clothes. She dragged herself upstairs and into the bathroom and ran the shower. The hot water stung her scalp. She closed her eyes in the hot stream, let it flood over her aching body, gradually warming her back to life. When, through habit, she stretched her hand out through the shower curtain it closed on to the soft warmth of a dry towel. Still there then, waiting for her. She wrapped it round her wet hair and went to find some clean dry clothes.

Her bedroom looked just the same. The bed was still made up. She rummaged in her drawer for clean underwear. She found a jumper and old cotton jogging trousers in Laura's wardrobe. More comfortable than her too tight jeans. Her fingers began to tingle, the warmth running along her veins, like something returning after a long absence.

Downstairs, through the open doorway into the dining room, she could see the answerphone light winking a message. She ignored it, went into the kitchen instead, turned on the light. She found a heel of bread and spread it thickly with butter. Turned on the kettle. Still eating, she wandered into the dining room. A stack of letters had been propped behind the clock. She pulled them out. Several, unopened, addressed to her. She took them back into the kitchen.

The heating was on; Dad couldn't be away for long. Suddenly ravenous, she put on a pan of water for pasta, settled at the kitchen table and opened the first letter.

It was from Will.

Outside, the dark garden filled up with snow.

Dear Mia,

I don't know if you'll get this. Perhaps your dad will post it on to wherever you are. It's weird not seeing you at school or anything. Becky told me what happened, about the hospital and you running away. Your dad has been here and talked for ages to my mother. I really hope you're all right. I never meant any of this to happen and I'm really sorry. Mum was so freaked out – but she's sort of on your side really. She made me write to you, but I don't know what to say.

I can't get it into my head about a baby. Mum said I should try to see it from your point of view, but it's hard when I haven't even seen you. I could have been prosecuted because you're only fifteen and it's against the law. My mother says the child-support agency can make me pay for it when it's born. What am I supposed to do, Mia? Leave school? Get a job? Mum won't hear of me leaving school.

I'm just in shock about everything. You must be too.

I got your postcard.
Will.

Her hands were shaking. She re-read it. What did he mean? It was disjointed, a muddle of different feelings. At least he'd written. Was still speaking to her. He'd signed his name, but it didn't say *love* or anything.

His mum knew. Everyone knew by now. All of Whitecross. Everyone at school.

Snow fell faster now, a sky full of feathers.

She opened the next letter. She didn't recognize the handwriting on the envelope and the letter inside had been typed.

Mia –

You are a brave young woman and have made a difficult choice, but at least it was your choice and I support you in that. I don't know you very well, and I wish I'd made more effort when you started going out with Will. Still, that's all water under the bridge.

I'll try and help you with money, because Will is responsible for this too and I don't want him leaving school or anything stupid like that. <u>Nor should you.</u> I've found out about special units for school-girl mums, where you can get on with your education. Get your exams. Get some support. There's one in Bristol. I've spoken to the head teacher already. I think that's where your mother lives, isn't it? So this

211

*might be a way forward for you. If you receive this
letter please get in touch. It can just be between you
and me.*

Sincerely,
Annie

Will's mother. Offering money. Help.

The next one was a print-out of an e-mail to
Dad.

*I have had two strange phone calls, one from a hos-
pital and the other from some very odd-sounding
girl. Please ask Mia to get in touch. Phone, letter,
e-mail, whatever. <u>Please</u>. Alice*

Car tyres crunched over gravel. Mia jumped up,
instinctively turned off the light so she could remain
hidden. Her whole body was tensed, waiting.

Door slam. Key in lock. Front door swung open.
Dad, mouth open, hair dusted white with fine snow,
stood on the mat. She knew he'd seen her straightaway, a small figure at the table in the dark kitchen.

Mia hesitated. 'Dad?'

He walked towards her and grabbed her into his
arms.

'You're freezing! You're all wet!' Mia's voice came
out squashed, crushed against his shoulder.

He hugged her again. Tears on his face, not snow-flakes.

It was going to be all right.

They sat quietly together in the kitchen. He didn't ask any questions. He seemed to know that it was better, for now, to say nothing. To share the moment together. Neither turned the light back on. The darkness was comforting; it softened everything. Through the window they watched the garden gradually transformed by the whiteness of snow. It smoothed over the rough flower beds, the clumps of bare twigged bushes. Rounded the edges of the fence, sculpted the grass and the paths into curves. The black branches of the ash tree blossomed with white furry buds.

'Magic,' Dad said. 'It's like a kind of magic.'

Mia's eyes glittered with unshed tears. Deep inside her, the frozen lump of fear and anger and hurt began to thaw.

Just before midnight, Mum's car slithered into the drive. It had taken her five hours since Dad's phone call.

Mia had been asleep, but she heard the engine and then the slammed doors and muffled voices as Dad let her in. It had been a long time since she'd heard Mum's voice in this house. It made her feel funny inside, listening to the voices drifting up. Like an old, old memory – lying in bed as a little girl, and the comforting sound of parents talking. Not the angry, shouting, miserable sort of talking they'd done before Mum left, but from earlier on, when they were still friends.

She strained to hear what exactly was being said, but they must have closed the kitchen door and, not long after, she heard Dad come back upstairs and go into his bedroom, and then Mum must have gone to the bathroom because she heard the sound of water running into the basin. She wondered fleetingly where Mum would sleep. Through the gap in the curtains she could see it had stopped snowing and the sky was clearing. A single star shone in the gap between the clouds.

CHAPTER TWENTY-FOUR

When she next woke up the room was full of the cold, white light of morning. Her parents were moving around downstairs. Someone had switched the radio on. She could smell toast. Mum came out into the hall and called to Dad in the kitchen.

'Shall we take it into the sitting room while we talk? The snowy garden looks lovely.'

Of course, there would have to be talk. About her. About what they were going to do with her. Mia felt the familiar flare of anger, but she was still so tired. All she wanted was to lie there and sleep.

When she finally got up the voices were still going on. The door was ajar. Mia sat on the top step and listened.

'– all over again. We're going round in circles.'

'But the school is there. She wouldn't be at home all day.'

'David, have you heard nothing I've been saying? This isn't going to work. Listen to me, for goodness' sake. You know how hard I found it. Impossible. I can't go back there again. I'm only just getting going again after that terrible time.'

'Well, what are you suggesting then? It's going to be all up to me again, is it? How on earth can I support Mia and a baby? All over again. Haven't I done enough?'

'I don't know. I really don't. It's hard for me to think straight right now. It's too raw, too much like what we couldn't sort out before, when it was *our* baby.'

'Why do you always have to bring it back to *us*? This is Mia we're talking about.'

'Because it *is* still about us, can't you see? What Mia's going through – it has everything to do with us. What we dumped on her. What I did. That's why I feel so terrible. Isn't it obvious? Her terrible hurt at me leaving. She wants a baby to love her, to fill the terrible yearning gap that's inside her, and maybe she's right. Maybe it will heal that old wound. Who are we to say? We messed it up. She'll probably do a much better job than we did. Than I did anyway.'

Mia sat with her head in her hands. Each word pierced her like an arrow. It was terrible to hear Mum's words, but she also knew they were true. *You*

have to face the truth. You can't go on pretending.
She did want a baby to love her, and for her to love.
It did feel like it might heal something for her. And
she did think she could do it better.

She walked slowly down the stairs and pushed
open the door. They both looked up. Mum had tears
on her cheeks. She tried to smile at Mia.

'Darling!'

'It's all right,' Mia told her. 'I heard what you said.
I just thought it might be better if I was here too,
since you're talking about me.'

'Yes. Of course. But can I just talk to you first,
Mia? Without David for a bit?'

She could see Dad biting back an angry reply. He
left the room abruptly, closed the door a little too
hard.

Mia felt cold again. This woman now sitting opposite her on the sofa was her mother. She didn't even
look how she remembered. Her hair was sleek and
dark, and she wore make-up, smudged a little now,
and smart fashionable clothes. She looked young.
Sexy, even.

'You're so thin, Mia! I'm so sorry. You poor love.'
Mia shrugged.

'I know you're still angry with me, Mia. You've a
right to be angry. It doesn't help you though, going
on and on, holding it to you like – like armour. It

hurts you more than anyone else. And now we've a baby to think about.'

Mia's hands tightened in her lap.

'Please, Mia. Can you just listen to me? Just for a short while hear what I want to tell you? I've thought about it so much, and if I don't say it now I probably never will.'

How could Mia say no to that? Her mother, pleading with tears in her eyes? But she couldn't smile. She didn't really want to hear what Mum was about to tell her. She could guess some of it already.

Mum read her silence as agreement. She fumbled to find the right words to begin with.

'It was a terrible, terrible thing I did, Mia. Leaving you and your sisters. I wouldn't have done it if I hadn't been desperate. I don't expect you to forgive me. I just think it might help if I tell you what happened. It broke my heart, leaving you all behind.'

'Why did you then?' Mia's voice was icy.

'In my muddled way I thought it would be better for you, that you'd be better off with Dad. He'd do a better job than me. He had his work and money, and he wasn't going crazy in his head like I was. It felt like the only thing I could do.'

Listen to the words. Concentrate. Eyes open. Breathe out.

'I thought I'd *die* if I stayed any longer, Mia. I was

withering, drying up so there was nothing left of *me*. Couldn't do it like everyone else seemed to. *Being a mother*. Anyway, at the lowest point I found I was pregnant again. A *fourth* baby. Too much for me, but too much for Dad too. He was working, no time, me ill, sicker than I'd ever been with the other pregnancies – and I'd been pretty bad when I was pregnant with you, Mia.'

No more. I don't want to hear this.

But Alice kept talking, even though Mia was a cold and ungiving listener, and gradually the story her mother told began to bind her in its spell.

'What could I do? I had three beautiful daughters. I knew what it was like to bring a child into the world, the birth, the magic of it. How could I not have this one? What kind of mother kills her own child? *"It's not killing. It's not a child, not yet,"* David said. He kept saying it. I think he was trying to help me out; he could see I wasn't in any fit state to have a baby – he wasn't either – and gradually I began to believe what he said, what other friends told me. That it wasn't so terrible, just a sensible choice, one that women have had to make for years and centuries even, taking control of their bodies.'

Her voice faltered. Mia leaned forwards ever so slightly.

'And then suddenly I didn't have a choice any

more. I began to bleed. A miscarriage. And it was all over. No baby. No choice. And instead, terrible guilt. That I'd made it happen. Terrible grief, over a lost child, except that why would I feel grief when I hadn't wanted it? I didn't deserve any sympathy. And after that, I couldn't bear to be around you all any more. Not David, or any of you children. All I could think was that I had to go away. By myself.

'I'm telling you this, Mia, not so you'll forgive me or anything, not to get sympathy, but because it's the truth of how it was, and because it seems important for you to know. It connects up with your story. The piece of ice you've kept inside you since then. It isn't yours, it comes from me.

'It's as if – this baby you've decided to have – it's a way to warm you again – from the inside – the child inside, coming to life – a way of loving again.

'I know we've still got lots to sort out, and it's going to be really hard, and maybe you'll end up thinking, I don't know, that it was the wrong choice. Sometimes, anyway. But you have made a choice and it's a brave one, Mia. You can be a good mother. Better than I've been.'

Heart thudding behind her ribs. Fear beating its wings. *Don't look at her. Don't show her anything.*

'Thanks for listening.'

'OK.'

'Anything you want to say?'

'No.'

Mum sighed heavily. 'Does it make sense to you, what I've said?'

'Yes. No. I don't know really.'

'Now we need to talk about you. What you want to do.'

'Yes.'

'Shall we call David back?'

'In a minute.'

'He's been a good dad, you know. Really good. I was right about that.'

'Yes. I know. You don't have to tell me that.'

In that second, Mia suddenly saw everything clearly.

'That letter you sent –' Mia looked directly at her mother '– it was horrible. I hated you.'

Alice was silent.

'Can't you see? I couldn't possibly go and find you after that, with the baby inside me, knowing what you thought. So I had nowhere to go.'

'I'm sorry, Mia. Again. I can't get it right, can I?'

'No.'

'You're better off here with Dad. Always have been.'

'Yes. And it's easier for you.'

'Don't be so hard, Mia.'

'It's just the truth, isn't it? You should face the truth. That's what you say.'

'Yes. I guess so. What about school and everything? There's a special place in Bristol and Dad thought –'

'I know. I could live with you. And go to the school. But you don't want me, and I don't want it either. Not now. I'll have to work something out.'

'I can help in other ways, Mia. With money, for instance. Now I've got a proper job. You heard about that, didn't you?'

'Yes.'

'Aren't you pleased for me?'

Mia shrugged. 'It's what you want, isn't it? It's nothing to do with me. I'll get Dad back in.'

CHAPTER TWENTY-FIVE

The baby is now completely formed. From now on, its time in the uterus will be spent in growing and maturing until it is able to survive independently of its mother.'

Now it was Saturday morning, and the house was full of people. Dad ruffled her hair every time he went past, grinning. It was after she'd said that she wanted to stay living with him in Whitecross that he'd started to smile, and he still hadn't stopped. She hadn't really thought before about what he might be going through. There hadn't been room for anyone else's feelings. Now she began to take in the truth that he'd loved her all the time. Even when he was furious with her. Disappointed, upset.

Over the next two days she told him, bit by bit, all that had happened. Almost all. She didn't tell him about Evie's baby, or the horrible, lurking fear that Evie had had a plan of her own, her own reasons for taking Mia on and looking after her. It had become a regular nightmare: waking, sweating, with the stomach-churning sense of something lost, missing. Not something, but someone. *You didn't want a baby, but we do.*

After breakfast, Dad telephoned Becky's mum, and then Will's mum, and then Miss Blackman. Mia grimaced when he called her *Julie*.

'You'll have to get used to it. Sorry, but you can't expect me to do without a love life forever.'

'But why her? A teacher. *My* teacher. She's not nearly good enough.'

'Well, at my age, you take it where you can.'

'Dad!'

Now they were all here, except Miss Blackman. She'd thought it better '*to leave the family to themselves for a bit*'. She did have some sensitivity then.

'Why do you have to invite them all over? They'll just go on at me.'

'To celebrate you being all right, silly. Coming home safely. They've all rallied round, helping me. They're not going to be making judgements, Mia. Not now. We've all moved on a bit. Can't you imagine what we've been through, worried sick about what might be happening to you, not knowing where you were?'

'Don't start again.'

'OK. We agreed. Anyway, *I* want to celebrate, OK? These are our friends, Mia. We're going to need them. You know that. We won't get through the next months without them.'

All these mothers. Becky's had brought pizza for everyone. Homemade.

Becky rolled her eyes at Mia. 'Can't we go upstairs?'

They lay on Mia's narrow bed. Just like old times. Almost. Becky lay on her side, propped on one elbow, and looked at Mia's stomach with her.

'You still couldn't tell though. I mean, maybe it's fatter than usual, but no one else would notice.'

'Have you seen Will?'

'At school, of course. Not much outside. No one's been going out much. Ali's given up on him. She fancies the new history teacher.'

'Oh no!'

'Well, you know her. She'd have had your dad if she could.'

'But Julie got there first. *Julie!*' They giggled.

'Your fault. You running off brought them closer together.'

'Depressing, isn't it?'

'Well, at least you don't have to go to school there any more.'

'No. I could go to the school-girl mother's place.' Mia wrinkled up her nose. 'If I wanted.'

'Do you?'

'Dunno. I'll go and see it probably. I'd have to live at my mother's place. Don't think I want to do that. Better here, with Dad. And you. And everyone. Even if it is a dump.'

'Good. I've really missed you, you know. She's not how I imagined her, your mum. *Alice*.'

'What do you mean?'

'Well, she seems really nice. Friendly. Attractive. I can't quite imagine her running off, leaving you all.'

'She talked about it the other morning. When she first got here.'

'What did she say?'

'It was awful. I was so tired – and I'd rather not know really.'

'Tell me. What did she say?'

Mia tried to explain. It didn't seem to make much sense now. She told Becky about the baby, the miscarriage.

Becky sat up on the bed. 'So when did she leave? How old were you?'

'Six. Nine years ago.'

'You nearly had a little sister. Or brother, I

suppose. They'd be about nine now. Weird, isn't it?'

A nine-year-old little sister.

But she hadn't stayed. Had taken flight.

Mia and Becky lay on the bed, listening to snippets of adult conversation drifting up the stairs.

'What about Laura? And Kate?' That was Alice's voice. *Mum.*

Laughter spiralled up from the kitchen.

Annie, Will's mother, said something about exams.

'They can wait. That's not the most important thing right now.'

Becky nudged her in the ribs. 'Did you hear that? That must be a first for your dad. Blimey!'

The door pushed open slightly and the cat padded into Mia's room. He stared up at them with his big round yellow eyes and then jumped on to the window sill. His jaw quivered involuntarily as he watched small birds hopping branch to branch on the tree.

'Silly old Apple Pie! He won't go out; it's too cold and wet. The birds know. The garden's covered in them this morning.'

'So, when will your baby be born, Mia?'

'May. I think. When you're all doing GCSEs.'

'But we'll still be around. To see you and that. I'll help you. It'll be amazing, Mia. We'll all help.' Becky had her dreamy look again.

'I guess.'

'What about you and Will?'

'I don't know. It sort of feels like it's nothing to do with him really. I know he's the father and that, but it was my choice, wasn't it, to keep the baby? I don't expect him – well – it's up to him to choose what he does, about the baby I mean. I don't want to force him into anything. It wouldn't work, would it?'

'I suppose not. But he's still its dad. You can't change that. And kids need both parents.' Becky flushed. 'Sorry, Mia. But they do. Even if you had to do without your mum.'

'She was there when I was really little. It was Dad who wasn't at first really. You know, always at work or working at home, thinking about other things all the time, not us. That's what Mum meant. That's what the trouble was with them; what it was like for her, doing everything.'

'Becks? Mia? Pizza's ready!' Becky's mother called upstairs.

They sat up again. Becky looked around Mia's bedroom critically. 'We'll have to do something about this room. You haven't changed anything in here for years!'

'Guess not. I can be your new project. You can re-design me, for your GCSE Textiles assignment. *"Room for a teenage mother and baby."*'

'Two rooms. Yours and a nursery. Stars on the

ceiling, and a sort of watery theme: seaside, with shells and starfish and a frieze of little crabs going round the walls.'

'Just one room actually. The baby will be with me. I'm not going to shove her off in another room all lonely-only.'

'Or him.'

'Well, yes, or him.'

'You can find out, you know. In advance.'

'I wouldn't want to. That would spoil it. You know, the first meeting.'

'We can think of names together! Make lists!' Becky was getting excited again.

Mia laughed out loud. She hadn't laughed like that for ages.

'Let's get our pizzas first.'

*S*unday morning. No one else was awake. Snow on the lane was rutted and stained rusty with car tracks. Melting snow slid from bramble branches and grasses along the road edge. On the footpath, shaded all day by overhanging trees, the snow still lay untouched. Mia's boots crunched. Each creaking step took her back. They hadn't had snow like this for years.

She was four or five years old. Mum stood at the open window, watching her three small daughters playing on the snow-covered lawn.

'*What are you girls doing? You'll be wet through!*'

'*We're making angels, Mum. We're showing Mia how.*'

'*Again!*'

'*Find a new space, Mia. Fresh snow. That's better. Then a big step, into the middle. There. Now flop straight back. Put your arms out. Swish them up and down for the wings. Now, carefully. Up. Don't tread on your angel.'*

'I did an angel!'

'You did! All by yourself. A little one.'

'The garden is full of angels. There's no more spare snow.'

Their field – Will's and hers – lay untouched by foot-steps. Just the light tracks of birds, and the deeper prints of a fox, perhaps. Will would know. That was the sort of thing he did know about.

The air was sharp on her face as she came out of the tree-sheltered path on to the track above the beach. She couldn't remember seeing snow on pebbles before. The sea was grey, moving in and out with a gentle shushing sound. Further along the beach towards Whitecross a child stood at the water's edge, chucking pebbles into the sea, too far off for her to hear the sound of stones plopping in, or boots crunch-ing over shingle. A flock of gulls swerved round in an arc, light reflecting off their wings as they turned.

Mia scuffed along the tide-line like she always did, half searching for treasures washed up by the tide, not really expecting anything. A pretty shell perhaps, or a bright skein of rope, a dried-up skate's egg pouch. Mermaid's purses.

The child had disappeared. Mia had the whole strip of beach to herself.

Her hands and feet were freezing. She walked faster, feet slipping on wet stones and seaweed. The tide was running out fast over the flat beach. As the sea drew further back, a gleaming strip of gravely sand was left behind. Mia's boots left soft prints that filled with water almost immediately and disappeared.

The clouds were thinning above the grey water. Between them stretched a slice of turquoise sky, fading to the palest, most delicate pastel blue. Baby blue. A thin curve of new moon floated just above the horizon.

Sometimes it turns out OK, of course. Once in a blue moon.

She bent down to pick up a small white feather, brushed it against her cold cheek. Soft as a new-born baby's downy head.

When she looked up she saw the child again, perched on a rock at the edge of the sea. Now she recognized the small, slight form, the wispy hair. Lainey! Her heart lifted. She waved and called out, but the wind snatched her voice away.

Mia began to run, her feet splashing up wet sand. She stretched her arms out wide, feeling the rush of cold air in her lungs. She was part of it all, the beach, the sea, the sky. Faster and faster she ran, right along the beach towards Lainey, the wind icy on her cheeks. For just this moment, Mia felt almost light enough to fly.

> *But once in a while the odd thing happens,*
> *Once in a while the dream comes true,*
> *And the whole pattern of life is altered,*
> *Once in a while the moon turns blue.*